FIRES OF THE HEART

Dreaming Brides of California Romance Series Book 1

KAT CARSON

KATIE WYATT

RoyceCardiff
Publishing House
WHOLESOME INSPIRATIONAL ROMANCE

RoyceCardiff
P u b l i s h i n g   H o u s e
WHOLESOME INSPIRATIONAL ROMANCE

Dear Reader,

It is our utmost pleasure and privilege to bring these wonderful stories to you. I am so very proud of our amazing team of writers and the delight they continually bring us all with their beautiful clean and wholesome tales of, faith, courage, and love.

What is a book's lone purpose if not to be read and enjoyed? Therefore, you, dear reader, are the key to fulfilling that purpose and unlocking the treasures that lie within the pages of this book.

NEWSLETTER SIGN UP GET FREE BOOKS!

http:/katieWyattBooks.com/readersgroup

THANK YOU FOR CHOOSING A INSPIRATIONAL READS BY ROYCE CARDIFF PUBLISHING HOUSE.

CONTENTS

A PERSONAL WORD FROM KAT   1
Prologue   3
Chapter 1   10
Chapter 2   16
Chapter 3   22
Chapter 4   31
Chapter 5   39
Chapter 6   48
Chapter 7   58
Chapter 8   68
Chapter 9   75
Chapter 10   82
Epilogue   93
ABOUT THE AUTHORS   101

Book 2: Rancher's Daughter

Book 3: Harvest of Love

PROLOGUE

Jasper, MO – Summer 1878

A COUGH TUGGED GABRIELLE UPWARD AND OUT OF A
dream. As she half woke, she realized that her own cough
had disturbed her sleep. Odd. She swiped at her sleeping
bonnet, grumbling over the rude awakening, and shifted
position on her bed. She coughed again. She frowned as
she dimly heard the sound of crackling. What was that?
Fully awake now, she rolled over to peer at her closed
bedroom door. What was that smell?

Was that—

She jolted upright, heart racing as she threw back the
covers and stepped from her bed, grunting with frustration as she tugged at the long white nightgown twisting
around her legs. She quickly stepped to her bedroom door,
wide awake now. She heard a shout from outside, followed
by a frantic pounding on the front door.

Something was wrong. Her fear growing, she twisted the doorknob and swung open the door, gasping as she inhaled smoke, provoking another cough.

A heavy, boiling cloud of smoke filled the short hallway, seeping in around the edges of the window that faced the narrow alley between her family's home and their bakery next door. The window glowed with flickering yellowish orange colors, confusing Gabrielle until she realized.

Fire!" she screamed. "Mama, Papa ... fire!"

Within seconds, her father pulled open their bedroom door and stared with dismay at the smoke as Gabrielle's mother appeared behind him.

"Quickly, Gabrielle, outside!" her father shouted.

In moments the heat grew hotter, the smoke thicker as they hurried out the front door. Without pausing, they ran next door to the bakery, flames licking at the roofing shingles, fingers of smoke curling around window frames. A small fire brigade had formed, men carrying buckets running toward the bakery from all directions, trailed closely behind by women in white gowns and woolen robes, their hair still covered with nightcaps, clasping blankets and buckets of their own.

Gabrielle stared at the bakery in horror, at the flames dancing in the second-floor windows where they kept all their supplies. She heard the pop and snap and hissing of flames as they found fuel, and even from twenty feet away, she felt the heat of the flames on her skin. Oh no, they had to save the bakery, their livelihood! Yet even in her panic, she knew it was lost.

Suddenly, her father darted down the narrow alley between the house and the bakery, reaching the side door of the shop.

"Stephen, no!" her mother cried, running after him.

"We've got to save what we can, Emily!"

Gabrielle stood frozen, watching her mother follow her father into the bakery. She started to move after them but a hand grabbed her arm. Heart pounding, a chill swept down her spine despite the heat emanating from the burning structure. She turned to find Marcus Hason, a deputy, staring at her, wide-eyed and face smudged with soot.

"Stay back, Gabrielle!"

She tried to pull herself free. "No, Deputy Hason, let me go! I have to help Mama and Papa!"

After a long, hot and dry summer, it didn't take but seconds before the upper floor of the bakery was engulfed in flames. They shot out the windows and licked at the eaves. Tendrils of smoke fingered the wood shingles, seeking more fuel and solid purchase. A breeze tugged at Gabrielle's hair and she watched wide-eyed as embers floated from the bakery to land on the roof of their small house next door. In seconds, the house, too, caught fire. Gabrielle choked back a sob, then cast another frantic gaze toward the bakery. Her parents hadn't come out yet. She managed to yank herself out of Hason's grasp and ran toward the bakery, ignoring shouts of warning behind her.

"Mama! Papa!" she cried frantically, squinting against the smoke, the stench of it filling her nostrils and choking her lungs. She lifted a hand over her mouth as she pushed open the side door and stepped into a smoke-filled room. The flames roared in her ears, growing ever more ferocious by the moment.

"Papa!" she choked out, then flew into a fit of coughing, nearly doubling her over. Her heart pounded hard, but fear propelled her forward. "Mama!"

A crash from above prompted Gabrielle to halt as she looked upward. A heartbeat later, the rear portion of the ceiling collapsed, sending a shower of flames and sparks and embers throughout the lower floor. So much smoke filled the bakery she couldn't see beyond her hands. Arms outstretched, she groped, fighting her panic and fear, assessing her surroundings.

"*Lord, help me!*" she cried. "*Save them!*"

She felt the edge of the counter that displayed their wares every morning; the breads, the biscuits, the pastries, and the cakes that Gabrielle, her mother, and father labored over day after day. Behind the counter was the workspace outfitted with two cast iron stoves with ovens, two wooden tables, and to the rear, the stairway leading to the upper floor where the supplies were kept.

She knew her parents must have run upstairs hoping to save some of their supplies and stock and equipment. Gabrielle once more tried to call out for her parents, but her throat felt scorched, her lungs on fire, and all she managed was a hoarse whisper. Her eyes burned … it was hard to breathe. She quickly moved forward, trying to ignore the intense heat, the lack of air. She reached the steps but stumbled on the bottom one and toppled forward. She landed hard, the side of her head banging into the wall.

"Mama ... Papa ..." she moaned, unable to speak louder, her voice a whispery croak.

She forced herself up, taking the steps one at a time, the fire *whooshing* around her with a furious life of its own, consuming everything in its path. She reached for the handrail but then snatched her hand away, hissing with pain at its heat.

"Gabrielle!"

Hope filled her heart when she heard the voice, but when it came again, she realized it was not her father ahead of her. The voice came from behind her, the voice of the sheriff, Andrew Flanagan.

She prayed that the townspeople outside had made some headway with the bucket brigade, but at the same time knew that they could do little to slow the ferocity of the flames hungrily feasting on the dry wood frame of the structure.

Above the pounding of her heart and the crackling of the flames, Gabrielle heard a sound. She froze, squinting through the smoke, seeking the origin of the sound. "Mama," she groaned just as a scream rose in pitch for several seconds and then abruptly stopped.

"No ... no, no, no ..." she refused to stop, refused to give up. Her parents were up there! They needed her help. She continued to scramble up the stairs, the risers and the steps charred, glowing like living things, pulsing with life, hissing and popping with laughter.

She ignored the heat, the threat of the stairs collapsing beneath her, sending her into the inferno now burning below. Gabrielle reached for the handrail once more to aid her in her climb, but at that moment, the stairs shifted and jolted downward a few inches. What breath she had caught in her throat. Heat surrounded her, consumed her, but she couldn't give up.

"Mama ..."

Suddenly, the stair structure crumbled from beneath her. A throaty scream escaped her as she flew downward and abruptly landed hard on something, then fell another foot. She tried to grab onto something but there was nothing to grab. The stairs collapsed completely from beneath her feet, flinging her down on the counter, and from there to the floor. Gabrielle couldn't catch her breath. Pain exploded in her body, the heat unbearable and the smoke so thick she couldn't breathe. Her chest constricted with the effort.

O Lord ...

Hands grasped her feet and tugged, pulling her back toward the side door and she dimly realized what was happening. Someone had come after her, trying to get her out. No! She had to save her parents! She couldn't leave them here! "No ..." she tried to cry out, but no sound issued from her swollen throat. Tears of despair flooded her eyes. She tried to fight but had no more strength. She was dragged out of the burning bakery, away from the smoke, the fear, the pain, all of it. Darkness overtook her and she sank into the bliss of oblivion.

CHAPTER 1

"*Be of good courage, and the Lord will strengthen your heart*," Gabrielle whispered, her voice still a scratchy whisper, her vocal chords singed by the heat of the fire. In times past, the verse, one of many songs of David, had brought her comfort, but now she felt nothing but empty and lost.

A hand settled gently on her shoulder and she glanced at her friend, sitting next to her on the porch of Agnes Weatherford's boarding house. The older woman had graciously offered Gabrielle a small room after the fire destroyed the Dawson family bakery and their home next door to it. Her parents had been buried four days ago.

"Be brave, Gabrielle," Olivia said, her voice tinged with sadness.

Gabrielle nodded and pulled her eyes away from what remained of the family home and business at the end of the street. Gone. It was all gone. She glanced down at her heavily bandaged arms and hands, resting in her lap. They didn't hurt so badly anymore, but just days ago the pain had been nearly unbearable, to the point that Doc had given her laudanum several times. After the first couple of days, Gabrielle didn't want the medicine any more. She believed that she deserved to suffer, to hurt in body and soul. She had failed to save her parents. She justified this pain.

"I know what you're thinking," Olivia said. "Every time you look down at your hands, I can see it in your eyes. You mustn't blame yourself, Gabrielle. It wasn't your fault. None of it was."

Gabrielle turned to look at her friend, blinking back tears. "I should've gone in right after them. I should've stopped them. I should've saved them."

Olivia slowly shook her head. "The fire was too hot, the damage already done. No one could've saved them. Take some comfort in what Doc said. The smoke would have made them unconscious before the fire reached—"

"Why?" Gabrielle interrupted with a frown. "Why would they do it? Why did they go in there?"

Olivia didn't answer because she didn't have an answer either. At times, Gabrielle felt furious with her parents for being so foolish, but then guilt overtook her, and then she again blamed herself for not going in after them sooner.

She slowly rocked in the chair, still numb from what had happened barely a week ago. The fire had taken everything she loved. Her parents, the bakery, her home. She glanced down at her hands. The fire had burned her hands and lower arms, Doc said. She would be badly scarred. She didn't care about the scars.

While her body would recover and the burns would heal, the doctor had also warned her that she wouldn't be doing any baking, or much of anything with her hands, in the near future. Gabrielle had a number of loving friends who had offered to take her in, but she had demurred. She didn't want to be a burden to anybody. It was only because Agnes insisted that she stay in one of her vacant rooms until she figured out what she wanted to do that she had accepted, but she had no way to repay the kindly woman. She couldn't even offer to clean rooms or help with laundry or the cooking.

"Am I useless then?" She turned to Olivia, lifting her hands. Even that small movement prompted shafts of pain to dart through her hands and up her arms, all the way to her elbows. She blinked back tears of self-pity. "What am I to do? If I can't use my hands, what am I to do? How am I to survive?"

"I already told you that you could come stay with me—"

"And do what? Sit in a rocking chair on the porch and watch life pass me by?" Gabrielle heard the bitterness in her gravelly voice and paused. "I apologize, Olivia. I'm feeling sorry for myself. It's just that ... everything's gone." She glanced once more at her bandaged hands. "What if I can't ... what if my hands don't ..."

Olivia squeezed her shoulder. "You've got to be patient, Gabrielle. Keep the faith. The Lord obviously has some plans for you, and I don't believe He's ready to take you just yet."

Gabrielle turned to her friend, lifting an eyebrow. "What are you talking about?"

Olivia smiled, shifted in her chair, and showed Gabrielle the Springfield newspaper that she'd likely gotten from the stagecoach office. Big-city papers were often left there by passengers moving through the small town of Jasper, located about thirty miles to the southeast.

"What is it?"

Olivia made a show of opening the newspaper and turning the pages until she reached the second to the back. Carefully, she folded the newspaper until it was no more than the size of a sheet of paper. "Read this."

Olivia held the paper up for Gabrielle. For several moments, she didn't know what she was looking at. Then, seeing the small subheading halfway down, she understood.

"Wanted ads for mail order brides?" Her eyes widened. "Are you insane?"

"Consider it, Gabrielle. A fresh start is what you need. This place is only filled with memories now, and nothing you can touch to link you to the past."

Her friend spoke gently but honestly. She was right. Nothing had been saved from the bakery or the house. No keepsakes, not even her parents' wedding rings had been found. The devouring fire had taken it all and left nothing but a pile of ashes. Still, a mail order bride? Gabrielle looked at her friend and frowned.

"And who would have me?" Gabrielle muttered softly, once more lifting her bandaged hands. "What can I offer to any man, let alone a stranger looking for a bride? Who wants a handicapped wife who can do nothing for him?"

Olivia sighed patiently. "Doc said that your hands would be handicapped only temporarily. As the burns heal, as scar tissue forms, you'll have some ability. Until then, let's be honest. You have no way to take care of yourself."

What Olivia said was true. Gabrielle glanced at her friend, offered a sigh and a shrug, and then gestured. With a grin, Olivia lifted the paper once more as Gabrielle and her best friend from childhood read through the ads. Maybe Olivia was right. She did need a fresh start, away from the horror, away from the guilt.

Her gaze returned several times to one ad placed by a man named Aiden Roberts. She read it aloud. "*Widower with two young children looking for a twenty- to thirty-year-old woman who loves children and is willing to move west to California.*"

"He's from a place called Maple Grove," Olivia said.

Gabrielle looked at her friend, her heart heavy. "It's so far away," she whispered, her eyes filling with tears at the thought of leaving her best friend. Her gaze passed over the town, deliberately skimming over what she could see of the remains of the bakery and her home. So far away. But maybe, God willing, California was the place where she could start over, where she might find a sense of renewed happiness and purpose.

<h1 style="text-align:center">CHAPTER 2</h1>

Sitting on a bench in front of the stagecoach office, the warm afternoon sun beating down on him, Aiden slid the letter from Gabrielle back into the envelope, wondering for the hundredth time if he had done the right thing. It had been six months since his wife Sarah had passed away from influenza. The illness had spread through California this past winter, carried west by pioneers, settlers, and prospective homesteaders along the trails, taking advantage of the transcontinental railroad the previous fall. Aiden's children, eight-year-old Rebecca and six-year-old Mary, needed a mother. He had no interest in love again, but he did need help raising his girls. He worked as the foreman on a neighboring ranch, hoping to someday save enough money to buy one of his own. For now, he lived in a small house on the northeast corner of the ranch property.

He missed Sarah. The girls missed their mother. Aiden tried his best, but the girls needed more stability. For now, they were shuttled around with friends during the day while he was at work, but he couldn't keep that arrangement forever. So far, those friends had turned away all offers of money or trade Aiden tendered for their help with the girls, but he couldn't take advantage much longer. They were his responsibility.

His brother Jared had written from Oregon and convinced him to place an ad for a mail order bride. Aiden wasn't sure it was the right thing to do, but he had few options left. He'd discussed it with his two good friends; Cody Maxwell, who lived on a ranch with his father nearby, and Jake Vance, who owned the town's mercantile store. While Cody felt much the same as Aiden did, that it was a quite extreme option, Jake reminded him that he didn't really have many options for marriage here in Maple Grove.

Maple Grove was a small town nestled in the hills of northeastern California, but it was a quiet town, not able to take advantage of railroads, shipping, or mining. All that was further to the west in San Francisco or south toward Los Angeles. There weren't many marriageable women in town or the surrounding area, and those Aiden knew would not be suitable for various reasons.

He sighed, once more looking down at the envelope and the scratchy handwriting on it. He and Gabrielle had shared several letters over the past two months, and she had been open and honest with him. She told him about the death of her parents in a fire, her injuries, and the fact that she was healing, but scarred.

He wasn't concerned much with scarring, but with her capability for caring for the children. The children were his only reason for taking such drastic measures. He shook his head. Things had certainly not gone as he and Sarah had planned. The influenza epidemic had taken them by surprise. Several townspeople had caught the illness and died from it besides Sarah, leaving a grieving Aiden and his two young daughters heartbroken and confused.

Still, placing an ad for a bride seemed ... wrong. It broke all the rules regarding courtship, engagement, and of course, the reason for getting married in the first place; falling in love, devoting oneself to another, with hopes and dreams and family.

Aiden already had a family. Rebecca and Mary. He'd had a wife. He wasn't really looking for someone to take her place. More like someone who was able to help with the children, cook, clean, do laundry ... but that sounded wrong too. He sighed. Gabrielle knew what she was getting into. She had been honest with him and he had been honest with her as well. Aiden had told her about Sarah, about the challenges of being a father trying to raise two children and hold down a job at the same time.

After the second letter he received from her, Aiden realized he had few options. After discussing it with Jake and Cody, he had proposed marriage to Gabrielle. She had accepted. The letter he held in his hand confirmed that she would be arriving this afternoon on the stage. He felt nervous, the hollow feeling in the pit of his stomach growing, his heartbeat accelerating with a combination of dread and relief as the stagecoach arrival grew closer.

"I don't want a new mommy," six-year-old Mary said, reaching for his hand.

Aiden glanced down at her, offering a smile that didn't reach his eyes. "She's going to help take care of you and your sister," he said. "She sounds very nice."

"I don't like her," eight-year-old Rebecca said, her jaw thrust forward, a frown emphasizing her comment.

Stubborn Rebecca and gentle Mary, two very different personalities, both of them taking after their mother. "We have to give her a chance, all right?" Aiden told them. He had to take his own advice as well. "Remember the proverb I read to you last night?"

"I don't 'member," Mary pouted.

Aiden smiled. *"The fear of man brings a snare, but whoever trusts in the Lord shall be safe."*

Rebecca looked up at him. "I'm not afraid," she said. "I just don't like her."

"Me neither," Mary mimicked.

Aiden sighed and squeezed both their hands. "This is something new for all of us. We need to be kind to Gabrielle, to show her hospitality and compassion. She needs us as much as we need her." The girls said nothing for several moments, and then Rebecca peered up at him.

"All right, Papa, I'll try."

"Me too," Mary grinned, sitting on the bench, swinging her legs back and forth.

Aiden turned and spied the dust cloud off to the east, and his heartbeat accelerated still more, his nervousness increasing. He took a deep breath, silently repeated the phrase he had just recited to the children, and stiffened his shoulders. What he'd said was true. He needed Gabrielle, and she needed them.

He and the girls watched as the stagecoach pulled to a stop, the horses stamping and blowing, sides flecked with sweat, trace chains rattling, and the springs of the coach squeaking as it settled. The coach driver waited for the small cloud of dust that floated behind it to dissipate before he wrapped long reins around the handbrake, then stepped down, the coach squeaking more as he moved to open the door.

Aiden waited anxiously. Had he done the right thing? Agreeing to marry someone he'd never met? What if they didn't suit one another? What if—

A passenger emerged. A woman. She wore a light blue cotton traveling dress and a dark blue woolen cloak that reached her waist. White lacy gloves covered her hands and arms all the way up to her elbows. She stepped down carefully, then looked up.

Aiden and his children remained silent. He glanced down at the girls, both eyeing the woman warily as he studied Gabrielle Dawson. She'd sent him a daguerreotype in one of her letters, a couple years old, of her and her parents standing outside the bakery. The image didn't do her justice. Of average height, her uncovered, dark blonde hair had been pulled back into a modest chignon. Aiden's heart skipped a beat as he stared at her heart-shaped face, softly rounded eyebrows hovering over hazel green eyes, and a small button nose.

Gabrielle took one look at him and the two children beside him and then walked toward him, her gaze studying him with as much curiosity as he studied her.

CHAPTER 3

GABRIELLE HID HER INNER TREMBLING AS BEST SHE could as she walked toward Aiden, her betrothed, and his two young children warily watching her approach. She tried to smile, not sure if she succeeded. Aiden Roberts was a tall man, standing a bit over six feet, with broad shoulders and a muscular build. He wore his thick chestnut brown hair slightly long, but was otherwise clean-shaven. Tanned from hours working in the sun, he had a square face, straight nose, and sapphire blue eyes. A handsome man. His lips curved upward with a smile as he extended a hand, palm up.

"Miss Gabrielle, I'm glad you made it to Maple Grove safely."

She slid her gloved hand into his for a quick and modest handshake, hiding the slight pain that even that movement brought her. She quickly slid her hand from his, a smile pasted on her face as she turned to the children. She knew they likely felt nervous and wary, perhaps even afraid. Well, this was something new to all of them, wasn't it?

"Hello, girls," she said, crouching down to be on eye level with them. "I'm Gabrielle."

Neither girl said anything. The younger one looked up at her father, eyes shining with tears.

"Mind your manners, girls," he said softly.

The older girl offered a slight dip of her knees and extended her hand as her father had. "I'm Rebecca."

Gabrielle smiled and lifted her hand again, their fingers barely touching as she nodded. "Nice to meet you, Rebecca."

"I'm Mary," the younger one said, hands clasped tightly behind her back.

"Hello, Mary, it's nice to meet you too."

She stood, knowing that it would take time for them to warm up to her. She hoped they would. Gabrielle glanced once more at Aiden and felt a flush warm her cheeks. A handsome and rugged man, he wasn't quite what she had expected. Then again, she probably wasn't what he had expected either. After all, there was only so much you could do in a letter to get to know someone.

She had told him everything in her letters and had been brutally honest. She had terrible scars on her hands and arms left by the fire. She had recovered some function in her hands, and the doctor had told her that over time, as she healed, she should regain more function and increased mobility.

The trip across country had terrified her, not because of the open, empty landscape or the miles that put her further and further from the only home she had ever known, but because of the big questions regarding her future. She knew she couldn't rely on the goodness of others forever but this 'adventure,' as Olivia called it, was terrifying. Even so, Gabrielle knew she had to find her own way in life, and so, after they had exchanged several letters, she had agreed to marry Aiden.

She had used the little bit of banked money from the bakery business for her travel arrangements, insisting that she pay for them herself so she wouldn't be instantly beholden to Aiden when she arrived. He had promised to marry her, but she was afraid that he might change his mind about that after he saw the scars.

"I've arranged for you to stay at the hotel tonight, as the preacher can't marry us until tomorrow. I hope that's acceptable."

Gabrielle nodded, suddenly feeling awkward. She wanted to stare at him, to take in every feature, to try and discern what kind of a man Aiden was as they stood there on the dirt street, the horses stomping impatiently as the coach driver heaved luggage from the top of the stagecoach and dropped it onto the ground near the rear wheel.

The movement caught Aiden's attention and he turned to look at her. "Do you have a trunk? Are those your suitcases?"

Without having to look, Gabrielle shook her head. "No, just a black valise," she said quietly. Her friends had given her some undergarments, stockings, two dresses, a skirt, and two linen blouses. The rest of her belongings ... her life, her hopes and dreams, had gone up in flames.

He glanced down at the children. "Wait here while I get her bag."

Aiden stepped away and Gabrielle looked down at the two children, staring unabashedly at her.

"Papa said that you got burned in a fire," young Mary blurted.

Gabrielle couldn't help but smile at her outspokenness even as her older sister sent her a glare.

"Mary," Rebecca scolded. "That was rude!"

Mary turned to her sister and scowled. "Well you wanted to know too, didn't you?"

Before Rebecca could reply, Mary once more looked up at her.

"Papa said your house burned down."

Pain stabbed Gabrielle's heart as she nodded, the little girl looking so innocently up at her. "Yes, it did."

"My mama died," the little girl blurted out suddenly. Her eyes glazed with tears and one spilled from the corner of her eye.

Gabrielle again crouched in front of the young girl. "Yes, I know, Mary. I'm very sorry."

Rebecca said nothing, standing stiffly beside her sister, still eyeing Gabrielle.

"We don't really want a new mama," Rebecca said.

The girl had spoken without malice or spite and Gabrielle's heart ached for her. "I know, Rebecca, and I—"

"Girls, that's enough," Aiden's voice spoke from behind.

Gabrielle rose and turned to find Aiden standing behind her, grasping the secondhand valise that contained all her worldly goods. He gestured with his chin toward the center of town.

"Let's go to the hotel so you can get settled into your room. We'll have supper in the dining room before the girls and I head back home."

Gabrielle nodded, once more feeling awkward and unsure. They were family and she was the intruder. It didn't matter that she was going to marry Aiden. It was an awkward situation for all of them, not just her and Aiden. He seemed to care for his children, but she'd only known him for a few minutes. What kind of man was he, really? What if he turned out to be contrary? What if he was overbearing and demanding? What if the girls never warmed up to her?

Gabrielle sighed, following Aiden. Maple Grove was a quaint little town, not much different from her own back in Missouri. Several passersby eyed her and Aiden, nodded wordless greetings, and moved on. A few lifted their hands and called out his name. He waved back. She gathered that he was liked here, which made her feel better. So did her quick view of the town itself. Windows were washed, the boardwalks swept, even the dirt of Main Street was leveled and smooth. Like the dirt streets back home, they were likely dragged several times a year to avoid deep ruts and large stones.

Mary held Aiden's free hand and Rebecca held Mary's. The children were beautiful, and based on Aiden's appearance, they took more after their deceased mother. Sadness once again nearly overwhelmed her and she stumbled slightly. She missed her parents terribly. She wanted her old life back. She wanted to be standing in the bakery right now, kneading cinnamon dough. She wanted it so badly she imagined the aroma of the cinnamon and the yeast. She wished a lot of things, as she was sure this young family did as well. Life was hard and full of challenges. Was she strong enough to meet hers?

The Lord works in mysterious ways, she thought. She wished she could understand what He had in mind for her and Aiden, both having suffered heart-wrenching grief and now, uncertainty. For now, she could only trust in the Lord and hope that she'd taken the path He wished her to take.

At that moment, Rebecca looked over her shoulder at Gabrielle, glanced down at the ground a moment, and then back again. Hesitantly, she reached her hand behind her for Gabrielle. With tears filling her eyes, Gabrielle took it.

AN HOUR LATER, AS THE SUN SLOWLY DESCENDED toward the western horizon, Gabrielle followed Aiden and the girls into the small restaurant attached to the hotel. She had gotten settled into her hotel room, washed up, and changed out of her traveling clothes. She'd donned fresh clothes, shaking out her skirt and blouse as best she could to remove the wrinkles. While she'd been occupied with that, Aiden and the girls had gone to the local mercantile, where he had promised each of them a licorice stick.

Now, as they moved into the dining room, Gabrielle's heart trip-hammered with anxiety. She had replaced her long white lace gloves with lightweight knit cotton gloves that slid easily inside the long sleeves of her blouse. Both Aiden and the girls glanced at the gloves.

They were seated at a small, square table in a corner of the dining room. It was fairly empty, as it was still relatively early in the evening for supper, and Gabrielle felt relieved when Aiden gave her the chair with her back to the room. Had he done that on purpose, so people wouldn't stare at her gloved hands? He made a show of holding the chair for all three of them, his girls giggling, and Gabrielle saw the adoration in their eyes when they looked at their father. They clearly loved him deeply.

She sensed that the girls were afraid that she was going to try to take the place of their mother, and she wanted to reassure them that was not the case, but it was too soon. They were likely as overwhelmed as she was tonight. A woman wearing an apron approached the table and she smiled at Aiden and the girls, then glanced at Gabrielle with open curiosity.

"Hello, Aiden, girls," she said, smiling. "It's good to see you. What can I get you tonight?"

Aiden glanced at Gabrielle a moment with a lifted eyebrow. She froze. Now came the hard part. She looked up at the woman. "Do you happen to have any stew?" She found trying to eat anything that required cutting was still extremely difficult and painful. It was nearly impossible to hold a piece of silverware, let alone use it properly. She didn't want to embarrass herself in front of her new fiancé and his children. Unfortunately, the woman shook her head.

"Sorry, ma'am, fresh out of stew."

Before Gabrielle could reply, Aiden spoke. "Steak and all the fixings for everyone tonight," he said with a smile, nodding at his girls and then sending a wink toward Gabrielle. "We're celebrating tonight," he finished.

Gabrielle was about to protest, but the girls squealed with excitement and she could do nothing more than smile even though her heartbeat kicked up a bit. Steak. She sighed softly. Well, maybe it was better just to get it over with.

She listened as Aiden made small talk with the girls and tried to include her in the conversation as often as possible, but with every second that passed, her dread increased. She wanted to make a good impression, wanted to show Aiden that she could be useful to him, that he wasn't getting ... she wasn't receiving charity from him. So why did he have to go and order steak?

CHAPTER 4

AIDEN WAS CAPTIVATED BY THE YOUNG WOMAN SITTING in front of him at the table. She was lovely, and he couldn't help but compare her to his deceased wife. He sensed that Gabrielle was a good person, and he admired her courage, traveling so far away from the only home she had ever known.

The food arrived and Gabrielle nodded her thanks to Maggie as she set the plate loaded with a T-bone steak and all the fixings in front of her. Maggie repeated the process with Aiden and the girls, the girls receiving smaller portions than the adults. Aiden immediately reached to cut the meat for Mary. Rebecca managed fairly well on her own. In addition to steak, which smelled delicious, their plates were piled with fresh green beans and quartered, roasted potatoes. Aiden's mouth watered as he watched Gabrielle slowly lift her hands and reach for her steak knife and fork.

She hesitated, and he saw her struggle to clasp the silverware. He glanced at her face, could practically see her willing her fingers to move. He saw a flash of pain across her features as her damaged nerves struggled to grasp the silverware but she lifted the steak knife and fork slowly in her hands, holding them awkwardly. She managed to pierce the corner of the meat and place the steak knife against it, but the moment she applied pressure, her fingers visibly weakened and the steak knife clattered to the plate.

Gabrielle swallowed and glanced up, her face flushed a deep red as Aiden and the girls watched her. She tried to laugh it off. "My apologies, I'm all butter fingers tonight."

Without responding to that comment, Aiden gazed at her, then glanced at Rebecca. "Hand me Gabrielle's plate, will you, Rebecca?"

Without hesitating, she did as her father asked even though Gabrielle gasped in protest. Without saying a word, Aiden made quick work of slicing her steak, cutting it into bite-sized pieces. He glanced at Gabrielle as Rebecca passed the plate back to her. Another furious blush colored her cheeks, along with a slight sheen of wetness in her eyes that she rapidly attempted to blink away. He said nothing, but continued making small talk with the girls.

Yes, he liked her. He sensed she was courageous yet quiet, a woman who bore her pain in silence. But he couldn't help but wonder how she was going to take care of his kids and his home if she could hardly use her hands. No one said anything for several moments, but after stabbing a green bean, Rebecca turned to her.

"Gabrielle, do your hands hurt?"

Aiden quickly glanced at Gabrielle and then his daughter. "Rebecca, hush."

"What happened?" Mary asked innocently. "How did you burn your hands?"

"Girls," Aiden began, but Gabrielle lifted her eyes to his and lifted an eyebrow.

"Maybe it's best that we just get it over with now," she said. "That way, if you change your mind—"

Aiden scowled. "Why would I change my mind? I'm a man of my word."

"I'm sure you are," Gabrielle said softly. "But these are … extenuating circumstances."

"Be that as it may, I don't think this is the appropriate time or place," he said quietly, aware that a couple of other guests had appeared in the dining room. Maggie emerged from the kitchen through a swinging door to take care of them.

Gabrielle glanced at the girls, then nodded. "All right," she said. "Girls, I promise to do my best to answer all your questions when your father says it's all right."

After several moments of silence, the girls returned to their food. All three of them tried not to pay much attention to Gabrielle's slow and laborious efforts to stab her fork into a piece of meat or a green bean, lift it to her mouth and nibble. Aiden hid a cringe, pity sweeping through him. She had gone through so much, endured so much, and she had nothing left. He knew by her posture and stoic expression as she ate that she was a proud and independent woman who had endured something horrible. Still, he had his doubts. She could barely feed herself. It was obvious that the function of her hands and fingers was severely restricted, most likely due to healing scar tissue.

How could he help but acknowledge the truth of the matter? He felt like a cad even thinking it, but how could she do the cooking when she could barely hold a fork? He'd been burned by a branding iron once and he remembered the sting of pain, the prickly sensation, the sensitivity to heat. How would she be able to bake? Do the laundry? It was obvious to him that it would be quite some time, if ever, before she could hold a needle and thread in her damaged fingers.

Though his appetite was gone, questions and doubts assailing him, Aiden forced himself to eat as if nothing were wrong. He chattered with the girls, darting occasional glances at Gabrielle, and couldn't help but wonder if he had just made a huge mistake. He hid a sigh and realized that he had to rely on his faith that he had made the right decision, that he was doing what was best for his children. God would guide their way. Aiden had to believe that.

After supper, they all went for a short walk. Night had settled over Maple Grove. The businesses on Main Street had closed for the evening, and on the streets behind, Aiden saw the glow of lights inside homes where families sat down to supper. He and Gabrielle walked side by side, the children scampering in front of them. He had questions, and he felt sure Gabrielle did as well.

To break the awkward silence, he discussed the schedule for the morning. "We'll go to the church at ten o'clock, where the preacher will marry us." Gabrielle said nothing, but merely nodded. "My home is a small place on the corner of the property of a ranch where I work. To date, the girls have been spending time with family friends and members of the congregation during the workday."

Gabrielle nodded, still saying nothing.

Aiden stopped walking and she paused beside him, the children moving a short distance ahead to pet a cat that meandered from the alley between a mercantile and a haberdashery. "Look, Gabrielle, I know this isn't going to be an easy change for any of us, but I want you to know that I'm going to give it my best."

"As will I," she said quietly, watching the girls.

"Do you want to change your mind?"

She looked at him with a wan smile. "Honestly, yes, but at the same time, no." She shook her head, turning from the girls to look at him before glancing down at her hands and slowly lifting them in front of her. "I'm going to be honest with you, Aiden. My hands don't work very well right now, but they're getting better. This is going to take some time." She looked once more at the girls and then back at him. "Here's the truth. I'm willing to take a chance on you. Are you willing to take a chance on me?"

Aiden thought about that for a moment. He wasn't looking for love. He wasn't looking to replace Sarah. He'd already endured one broken heart and he wasn't about to risk a second go-around. "You're being honest with me, so I'll be honest with you. I know you told me about your injuries, but I just didn't realize they were so ... so severe."

"I understand, but—"

"Let me finish, please." He looked at his girls and then back at her. "The girls need a mother. I need someone to help look after them, make sure they're safe, and ensure that they continue their learning. I want them to have a sense of security when I'm not around. I'm usually working dawn to dusk. I have most Saturdays and Sundays off, for church and whatnot. If you say you can handle that, I believe you, but I want you to know that the safety of the girls is of the utmost importance."

She looked up at him, her eyes searching, looking for what?

"I understand," she said quietly.

"Papa, you said we could talk to Gabrielle after supper. Can we?"

Aiden glanced down at Mary, her eyes wide, her face so lovely and innocent as she reached for his hand, eyeing Gabrielle with a wary expression. He watched as Rebecca also approached, then at Gabrielle. At her answering nod, he offered a sigh and a shrug. "Ask away."

Both girls started at the same time. Aiden chuckled and told Rebecca to let Mary go first. The eight-year-old was nothing if not blunt.

"How did you burn your hands?"

"In the fire you asked me about before," Gabrielle answered simply.

"But how?" Mary pressed, visibly confused. "My mama wouldn't let Rebecca and me go near the stove when there was a fire burning in it. Did you burn your hands on the stove?"

Gabrielle smiled sadly down at Mary and shook her head. "No, Mary, I didn't burn my hands on the stove." She glanced at Aiden and then continued. "My parents and I lived in a house that was connected to our bakery—"

"You make breads and pies and biscuits?" Rebecca interrupted.

Gabrielle smiled at her. "Yes, Rebecca, we also made cakes and cookies and all kinds of delicious things."

"So what happened?" Mary asked, not to be put off.

"There was the fire. My parents ran into the bakery. It was burning, and ... anyway," she said, lifting her gloved hands. "I tried to save them, and that's how I burned my hands."

"Did you?" Rebecca asked.

"Did I what?"

"Did you save them?"

Aiden saw the wince that Gabrielle tried to hide as she slowly shook her head. "No, Rebecca, I didn't."

The girl said nothing after that, exchanged glances with her father, and then looked back at Gabrielle. They now understood what had happened. Mary glanced up at Aiden, tears once more brimming in her eyes. He knew she was thinking about her mother. The girls missed Sarah terribly, as did he.

"Come on, girls, it's time we let Gabrielle get some rest and then I'll get you home and put you to bed. We have a big day tomorrow."

CHAPTER 5

Two weeks had passed since Gabrielle had married Aiden. Two long and frustrating weeks. She often felt like a fish out of water, left to her own devices, expected to fill a role that she had never played before. Wife. Mother. The girls were well-behaved, so it wasn't that. It wasn't even the fact that Aiden was gone much of the time. While the girls were polite, they kept their distance. Gabrielle wasn't sure whether it was because they were afraid her scars, which they had seen because she couldn't keep her hands and forearms covered all the time, or if they were afraid she was trying to take the place of the mother. She had assured them that that wasn't the case, but they refused to call her anything but Gabrielle, which was fine with her at this point.

Truth be told, Gabrielle felt more alone now than she had back in Missouri. Around people, but not really included in their lives. She was expected to provide supervision for the children and perform household tasks, which took her two to three times as long as they had before she had been so badly injured.

Back in Missouri, she had often helped her mother make soap. She had also done laundry, cooked, cleaned, and ironed, but it seemed to her that every task now was impossibly painful and difficult. Her hands didn't want to work properly, and sometimes shooting pains in her injured fingers made her want to cry. Of course she didn't, but the discomfort was ever present.

Even though Gabrielle and Aiden were married and shared the same bed, he had yet to even touch her. He had yet to kiss her. Usually, he waited until she was in bed and asleep before he joined her, and he was always gone before she woke. Not that she expected romance this early in the marriage. They were strangers after all. Yet he didn't seem inclined to remedy that. Aiden was gone before sunup most mornings except Sunday, and home by suppertime. After supper, he played with the children for a while, then sent them to bed. Then, he took up his usual position in a chair before the fireplace, reading the newspaper, his Bible, or sometimes, the almanac.

He rarely engaged during conversation other than to ask about the children. Gabrielle wasn't sure, but he seemed preoccupied, mumbling one- or two-word answers to questions she had. On occasion, she felt him watching her, but when she turned to look at him, thinking that he might want to talk, he turned away.

She didn't know how to deal with it. She didn't know what to expect of him. She was attracted to him and she didn't try to deny it to herself. Did she want him to kiss her? Did she want him to court her? She didn't know. He'd been married before. She didn't know what to expect. None of her friends back home had been married so she had no reference in regard to expectations. Her parents had never been so quiet together, not even when they disagreed about something. They constantly laughed, talked, and sometimes argued, but they were true partners in all ways.

Thinking of her parents brought tears to her eyes. Gabrielle missed them terribly and wished she could ask her mother for advice. She might have moved thousands of miles away, but her memories were never far from them, nor were thoughts of her former life, and the growing belief that she had made a huge mistake coming out west and marrying a stranger.

Ashamed, Gabrielle closed her eyes and mentally recited a portion of the Sermon on the Mount, *"Look at the birds of the air, for they neither sow nor reap nor gather into barns; yet your heavenly Father feeds them. Are you not of more value than they?"* Yes, the Lord had brought her here and she must trust in Him. She must. Yet, she felt uncertain and often afraid.

Maybe she should bring up her doubts and fears to Aiden. Maybe they could talk about it. Gabrielle sighed. Tonight, as usual, Aiden sat in his chair by the fire while she finished up washing the dishes. Even that was a laborious task, her fingers finding it difficult to grasp a plate, a mug, and even the dishrag. At times, the pain that shot up her arm brought tears to her eyes, but she blinked them away, refusing to show weakness in front of Aiden or anyone else.

Aiden muttered softly and she turned to him, eyebrows raised in curiosity. Had he seen her fumbling with such a simple task? Her own mood souring, she stepped toward him and spoke. "Is something troubling you, Aiden?"

He glanced up at her from a piece of paper he held, then frowned. "What? What makes you think something is wrong?"

"You're mumbling" she replied. She didn't want to push him, but it was time to clear the air. "Is it something I'm doing? Or something that I'm not doing?"

What?" He paused a moment and then shook his head. "No, Gabrielle, it's not you." He gestured to the paper in his hand. "It's about work."

"What about it?"

"Some supplies have gone missing from the ranch where I work." He frowned. "Actually, there have been a number of issues at the ranch and in town that just don't make sense."

"Like what?"

"Someone broke into Jake's Mercantile and stole some things last month. A few weeks before that, someone broke into the bank late one night and tried to rob it. They didn't get into the safe though."

Gabrielle frowned. She'd thought Maple Grove was so safe. "But what does that have to do with you?"

Again a sigh. "My boss, the ranch owner, thinks I'm not doing my job properly, that I should have caught the person stealing things."

"Isn't that the sheriff's job?"

Again he shook his head but said nothing.

"Anything I can do to help?"

"No, it's work. I'll handle it."

Gabrielle was still curious, but even more importantly, she wanted to see how much he was willing to confide in her, or not. "But you'll tell me if I can help, won't you? I helped my parents run our business. I know some things about—"

"Nothing for you to be worried about."

Aiden turned from her, the conversation over, effectively dismissing her. Gabrielle bit her lip in annoyance, wanting to ... to what? Demand that he treat her like a wife and not merely a housekeeper? That he confide in her? That he act like she was his partner? That their relationship was more like the one her parents shared? Gabrielle shook her head and stepped back into the kitchen, quietly putting the dishes away.

It was growing late and the children were already settled in bed. She reached for the kerosene lamp on the kitchen table, figuring she might as well go to bed as well. Tomorrow was laundry day, a huge challenge for her with her injuries, but a task she was determined to complete. She stepped from the kitchen and into the main room, starting down the hallway when suddenly the lamp slipped from her grasp. She gasped, uttering an alarmed cry as the lamp crashed to the floor, shattering. The air filled with the scent of kerosene, small flames igniting the puddle on the floor, reaching for the hem of her skirt. Aiden jumped up with a shout as Gabrielle stared, frozen, down at the small flames burning the hem of her dress. The horror of the fire that killed her parents came back to her in a rush. The heat, smoke, the pain. She panicked and screamed.

The children emerged from the room, eyes wide, taking in the scene with a glance. Mary burst into tears.

"Back to your room!" Aiden shouted. "Shut your door!"

They obeyed while Aiden reached his coat, hanging on a wooden hook by the door. He quickly threw the coat over the flames on the floor, stomping them out, then turning to Gabrielle and repeating the process on the bottom of her skirt. It was all over in a matter of seconds. Gabrielle stared at the mess, filled with shame as he stared at her. He didn't have to say a word.

She felt worse than useless. Would he send her away now? Would he have the marriage annulled? Would he—

"Papa!" Rebecca's voice came from the children's bedroom. "Papa, can we come out?"

Aiden glanced down at the floor, made sure that all the flames were out, and then replied, "It's all right, children. Yes, you can come out now."

Rebecca appeared, tightly clinging to Mary's hand, both of their faces pale, eyes wide as they stared. "What happened?"

"It's all right, Rebecca. You girls can go back to bed. Gabrielle dropped the lamp. It's all right now."

Gabrielle, her face flushed with embarrassment, looked at the children. "I'm sorry I frightened you." She tried to smile with assurance, but failed. Was that look Rebecca sent her one of accusation or had she imagined it? Mary still cried softly and Gabrielle wanted to comfort her. She stepped toward the child, but Mary cringed and hid behind Rebecca.

"Go back to bed, girls," Aiden said, moving toward the kitchen. "I'll have this cleaned up in a minute."

"It stinks," Rebecca said.

"Go back to bed," he repeated. The girls retreated, closing the door softly behind them.

Gabrielle turned, also moving toward the kitchen. "I'll help."

"No, I've got it."

Gabrielle swallowed hard and remained where she was. "I'm sorry, Aiden. It was an accident—"

"I know that, Gabrielle," he said, turning toward her. "But you've got to be more careful. If I hadn't been home ... "

He didn't have to say it. Blinking back tears, Gabrielle wanted to promise him that it would never happen again, that she would be more careful, that she wasn't useless. She couldn't help feel that way. She had scared the children. She had scared Aiden. She had scared herself. If he hadn't put the fire out as quickly as he had, it could've been a lot worse. She had frozen, traumatized by the sight of flames licking at her skirt. Traumatized by the memory of roiling smoke, choking, the acrid stench, the pain she had endured ...

"Go to bed, Gabrielle," he repeated. "We'll talk about this more tomorrow."

Gabrielle retreated to their room, telling herself not to cry. Do not cry! She closed the door softly behind her, lowered her chin to her chest, embarrassed, humiliated, and frightened. *O Lord, give me strength*! What would she do if Aiden sent her away? What if the children never learned to trust her? What if Aiden ...

Oh what was the use? She knew why Aiden had brought her here and married her. He had made it clear in the beginning and she had agreed. It was foolish for her to expect a romantic and loving relationship such as her parents shared. How could she? She and Aiden had never courted. They had not gotten married out of love but out of necessity. Even so, Gabrielle wasn't holding up her end of the bargain. She couldn't care for the children, couldn't even perform the most mundane household chores. So what value did she bring him?

She lifted her chin, stiffened her spine, and refused to feel sorry for herself any longer. She told herself she was still healing, that her hand movements would not be limited forever. And yet, it had been a couple of months since the tragedy. How long would it take for her to recover the use of her hands? How long before Aiden or the girls grew tired of her handicap?

She heard Aiden sweeping up the shattered glass in the hallway and wanted to go out and help him, to insist that he allow her to help, but at the moment she lacked the courage. What she wanted was assurance. Some words of comfort. Maybe even a hug. How long had it been since she'd been hugged? She wanted a true marriage, in heart, body, and soul. She sighed. Tomorrow was another day.

She gazed down at her hands in the darkness, ordering them to heal, trying to curl her fingers inward but biting her lip against the pain. She would improve her stamina. She would practice grasping things. She was determined to be a good wife, a good mother, and to overcome the obstacles in her way.

She would. Gabrielle just hoped that Aiden and the girls could be patient enough with her. That they would give her time to prove it. That she could be a good wife and mother, no matter what it took.

CHAPTER 6

Two weeks had passed since what Gabrielle had termed the 'incident'; the evening she had dropped the kerosene lamp in the house. After that, there had been no accidents, at least those that Aiden knew of, and his girls hadn't mentioned anything either. The girls were slowly warming up to Gabrielle, and he couldn't deny that he liked her too. He often watched her, the way she moved, the way she blew her hair from her forehead when a stray tendril escaped the loose bun she wore it in. He knew she couldn't manage more than that.

He admired her courage and her determination to work through her obvious pain. While he still had his doubts whether things would get better, either with Gabrielle or his current situation, he wasn't sure. At this moment, all was debatable. In addition to his worries about his family life, Aiden also struggled with difficulties with his job as foreman at McGregor's Star Feather ranch.

"So what does Mike McGregor say about it?"

Aiden pulled himself from his thoughts and turned to Jake as they sat in the storeroom of his mercantile. The front, side, and back doors were open, allowing fresh air to get in and hopefully cool down the increasing heat inside the building.

"Not much," Aiden shrugged. "But over the past couple of weeks, odd things have been happening. Harness and tack missing, the small pond at the rear of the property contaminated—"

"Contaminated with what?" Jake interrupted.

Aiden frowned. "Salt. Can you believe it? I found two empty ten-pound burlap sacks for salt lying in the bushes behind the watering hole. It'll take a couple of good, hard rains to make it drinkable again. I had to fence it off yesterday so the livestock wouldn't get into it." He shook his head. "Who would do something like that?"

Jake shook his head. "I have no idea. Do you?"

"No," he said. "But I have a feeling that McGregor has his suspicions."

"Really? Who?"

He looked at his friend. "Me."

"You?" Jake exclaimed, eyes wide. "Why would he think you have something to do with it?"

Again, Aiden shrugged. "I don't know, but it worries me. If I don't find who's responsible, and soon, I'm afraid I'll be out of a job."

Jake said nothing for several minutes, both of them staring out the door of the storeroom, watching occasional passersby, riders on horses, and wagons rolling by.

"How are things at home? How's Gabrielle getting on? The kids warming up to her any?"

Aiden heaved another sigh. "I think she's starting to win them over, but I'll tell you, the first time they got a good look at her hands and arms ..." He had told Gabrielle that they might as well get it over with, that the longer they put it off, the longer it would take for the kids to deal with it.

The moment Gabrielle had pulled off the gloves, Mary had gone completely pale and her eyes wide, then she had scrambled into Aiden's arms, hiding her face in his shoulder. Rebecca, on the other hand, had stared wordlessly for several moments. Finally, she asked Gabrielle a question.

"Will those wrinkles go away?" she asked, trying to hide a grimace of revulsion, without much success.

Aiden looked at Gabrielle, saw the sadness in her face, and she, too, gazed down at her injured limbs. "They're called burn scars," Gabrielle explained softly. "No, they won't ever go away. Some of them might smooth out some, but I'm afraid I'm stuck with them for the rest of my life."

Aiden had felt bad for her, to have such a permanent reminder of her pain, her grief, and her loss. He spoke gently to the children. "You remember what Mama and I told you, that in order to take stock of any person, you have to look beneath the surface?"

Rebecca nodded somberly and Mary lifted her face from his shoulder. "She told us that everyone is one of God's children, some different than others. Some can do things that others can't, and we're supposed to treat everyone with kindness."

Aiden glanced down at his daughter, proud that she remembered. He had hoped that little Mary wasn't too young to remember her mother. He smiled. "That's right, honey. We're all different, but we're all God's children."

Rebecca looked at Gabrielle then, her eyes somber and her expression serious. "Can I touch them?"

"Rebecca—"

"It's all right, Aiden," Gabrielle interrupted. She gazed down at Rebecca with a small smile. "Yes, you can touch them."

"I won't hurt you, will I?"

"As long as you don't try to squeeze my fingers, you won't hurt me."

The three of them watched as Rebecca skimmed her small fingers gently over Gabrielle's, then along the back of her hand, tracing one wicked-looking and raised burn scar over the corrupted skin of Gabrielle's forearm. Some places were still dark red, others pink, others blotchy white and shiny. The child shuddered softly, then continued, watching Gabrielle the entire time.

Aiden felt a surge of affection in his heart watching Gabrielle's patience with his girls. But it was the very fact that he admired her and found her attractive that scared him. His heart had already been broken. He wasn't going to fall in love with Gabrielle. He refused to.

"Aiden?"

Jolted out of his thoughts, he turned to his friend. "There haven't been any more accidents, and I may sound callous and uncaring to say this, Jake, but I'm not sure about ..." He swiped his fingers through his hair. He needed to get it out. "She can't do a lot of things yet, and what she can do, she often struggles with. It takes her two or three times as long to complete a task as it would someone else."

Jake said nothing for several moments. "But she's trying?"

Aiden nodded.

Jake clapped a hand on his back as he rose. "Give it time, Aiden," he said. "I know you had expectations, but she was honest with you from the beginning."

Aiden looked up. "Yes, she was honest, but I didn't expect the injuries to be so severe that she couldn't—"

The sound of someone entering the mercantile compelled Jake to pull his attention away. Before he left the store room, he smiled. "Be patient. Give her time. I have a feeling that before you know it, you'll settle into your new lives together. But to get there you have to be honest with her and she has to be honest with you. Talk to her. Get to know each other. Let her know what you're thinking, what's going on at the ranch, your concerns."

With that, he turned away. Aiden sat for several moments, considering his words. He knew that Jake spoke the truth. Honesty was important in any relationship, and he hadn't been sharing much of himself with Gabrielle over the past month. He couldn't expect their relationship to blossom like it had with Sarah. He was older, the circumstances were completely different, and so, too, were his expectations.

For the first time, he put himself in Gabrielle's shoes. Would he have been brave enough to move thousands of miles away from the only home he had ever known? Could he have moved away from Maple Grove as she had from her hometown? A different state, not knowing anyone, relying on the kindness of a literal stranger to provide a small sense of security? She had come here looking for a future. She had come here looking for a new life. And how had he treated her? Aiden wasn't treating her like a wife. He was treating her like a housekeeper, nanny, a cook, and a laundress. He had never treated Sarah that way. They had shared their hopes and dreams, their fears and their successes.

Gabrielle could be walking on eggshells, afraid to do the wrong thing, afraid to make another mistake for fear that he would send her away. And if Aiden did, where would she go? He determined that he would strive to be more open and honest with her. He had to express his concerns, as did she. With that resolve, he reached for his hat, slapped the dust from it, crammed it on his head, and left the mercantile. Time to go home.

THAT NIGHT, AFTER THE CHILDREN HAD GONE TO BED, Aiden did his best to open up to Gabrielle. She sat on the bed and let her hair down, then awkwardly grasped her brush. He left the threshold of the door and moved toward her, reaching to gently take the brush out of her hand. She glanced up at him in surprise and he grinned.

"I can help brush your hair, Gabrielle. I know it's a struggle." He noted her hesitation and his grin broadened. "I've gotten quite good at it, actually, what with doing Rebecca and Mary's hair every morning."

She offered a small nod and sat stiffly as he began to brush her hair from the bottom up. After a few moments, she relaxed. As Aiden brushed, he spoke, he took Jake's advice and addressed his concerns, many of which she agreed about. She knew her own current limitations. She also took the opportunity to confide in him.

Gabrielle gazed down at her now gloveless hands, lifting them before her. She tried to spread her fingers wider and winced. "You've been honest with me, Aiden, and I shall be honest with you. It's growing increasingly difficult to move my fingers at all. It's like they're stiffening up." She showed him, trying to curl her fingers inward, but only managed to move them maybe a fraction of an inch. "I thought they'd get better as I used them."

"We have a new doctor in town. He's young, from back east. Maybe you should go see him. His name is Micah Harris."

She frowned. "Doctor visits cost money," she said, shaking her head. "Besides, he can't perform miracles. I doubt he can do anything about these." She looked over her shoulder at Aiden. "I'm truly sorry that I haven't been the wife you bargained for. I—"

Aiden reached out and placed a gentle hand on her arm, his fingers curling around scar tissue there without a hint of revulsion. She stared at him in dismay. "We'll get through this, Gabrielle, all of it. The trouble at the ranch and with your hands." He smiled. "Tomorrow, I need to go to McGregor's for a few hours in the morning, and then I have the rest of my Saturday and Sunday off. After I finish tomorrow, we'll pay a visit to young Dr. Harris and see what advice he can give us."

Gabrielle didn't look too sure, but she managed a smile and a nod. For the first time since she had arrived, Aiden felt a surge of hope that they could make their relationship work. He'd already seen his daughters opening up to Gabrielle. Maybe, God willing, things would eventually work out.

THINGS DIDN'T WORK OUT AS AIDEN HAD HOPED. THE morning started off hot and grew hotter. Grasshoppers flitted across the dirt path as he rode the meandering trail over the hills from his small house to the bunkhouse on the ranch, looking forward to completing his tasks, one of which was to ensure that the ranch hands would be ready to start branding come Monday morning.

He smiled with satisfaction as he recalled the discussion he'd had with Gabrielle the night before. Jake was right. Talking with her and being honest had made a huge difference. It was amazing what a little bit of communication could accomplish. Everything had been so easy with Sarah that they hadn't even had to think about such things. But he had to constantly remind himself that Gabrielle wasn't Sarah.

When Aiden arrived at the ranch, he was surprised to find McGregor in the front yard, scowling. A couple of ranch hands stood beside him, all of them looking off to the east. He rode up, dismounted, and followed their gaze, seeing nothing.

"What's going on?" he asked. He was startled by the scowl McGregor gave him, his eyes flashing in anger, and his tone of accusation as he replied.

"Two of my cattle were found slaughtered in the east pasture early this morning, Roberts! Gutted them! Whoever did it didn't even have the gumption to take the meat, just cut the cows open and left the meat to spoil!" He jabbed a finger at Aiden. "This is your doing!"

Aiden's eyes widened. "Mine?" A surge of anger boiled upward. "What would make you think I had anything to do with this?"

One of the ranch hands looked at him, and then, following a nod from McGregor, extended his hand and showed him what he held.

"That was found near the slaughtered cows, Roberts. You want to tell me that this isn't yours?"

Aiden stared in dismay at the pocket watch the ranch hand held out toward him. His mouth grew dry and he frowned in confusion as he stared at the initials engraved in the silver cover plate.

A.R.

He frowned, looked up at McGregor, and protested his innocence. "That's my pocket watch, but I have no idea how it got out there. I haven't been to the east pasture in the last couple of days!"

McGregor's face turned red as he shook his head, jabbing his finger toward Aiden's horse. "You're fired, Roberts. Get off my property this moment before I decide to just shoot you!"

CHAPTER 7

GABRIELLE STARED AT AIDEN IN SHOCK AS HE TOLD HER what had happened at the ranch and that Aiden had been ordered off the property. Frightened, she wondered where they would live. The children were outside, gathering eggs and finishing their morning chores. Her heart thudded dully in her chest as she tried to comprehend it all. What else could go wrong?

"How long is this been going on?" she asked.

"A few months. At first it was thefts of odds and ends, but in the past few weeks it's gotten worse. I tried to talk to old man McGregor about it, but he won't … He and I both think that someone's trying to damage his ranch and property. He isn't the only one. Several other farmers and ranchers have complained to the sheriff about thefts and damage."

"But McGregor thinks it's *you*?"

Aiden nodded.

Gabrielle didn't know what to think. She didn't know Aiden that well yet, but she felt certain that he would never do such a thing. A man as dedicated to his children as he, one who was so kind and gentle with them, couldn't do something like that. Why would he? As foreman, he lived in this house on the ranch owner's property, free and clear. He kept it nice, in good repair, and well-stocked. Why would he endanger that?

"There it goes," he sighed, staring out the open door toward the yard.

"There what goes?"

He turned to her, slowly shaking his head.

"I've been saving as much as I could, every spare penny, hoping that someday I could save enough to buy my own piece of property, build my own ranch. The land out here is pretty cheap. Actually, there's a nice bit of property some ten miles out from Maple Grove that I've been keeping my eye on. I claimed the property at the assay office and marked out some property lines. I was able to finagle a small loan at the bank to put down enough money to make my claim official. Problem is, if I don't come up with the other half of the money by the end of the year, I'll lose it."

"So what happens now?" She didn't ask the words that she dreaded most of all. Now that they no longer had a place to stay, would he send her away? Was she just another burden, one more mouth to feed?

"Aiden, what are we going to do?" she asked.

He shrugged.

"I'm thinking on that." He paced the room for several moments before he stopped and turned to her. "Let me talk to Cody Maxwell, a friend of mine who lives out on a farm with his father south of town."

Gabrielle couldn't recall a Cody Maxwell. She had met Aiden's other friend, Jake Vance, the owner of the mercantile.

"Never mind, I can't ask Cody to put us up. He's got his hands full with the farm and can't afford to hire me on. I don't know much about farming anyway. I know how to take care of horses and cattle and ..." He paused, swiping his fingers through his hair, frowning with frustration. "Besides, he doesn't have any place there that we could stay and I don't want to take anyone's handouts."

In that way, Aiden was much like her, Gabrielle thought. Neither of them were comfortable with charity. Of course, it wasn't just a matter of pride, as the Bible said that pride goeth before the fall. She knew, from what Aiden had told her and from what she'd experienced in a couple of church services herself, that the people of Maple Grove were kindhearted, generous people. She knew he wouldn't want to take advantage of any of them, even for a short time. What made the matter worse was that Aiden had been accused of theft and the slaughter of two of McGregor's cattle. Gabrielle might be from Missouri, but she knew that thieves and rustlers were not thought of kindly anywhere. That thought prompted a chill to run down her spine.

"Aiden, do you think McGregor will ... do you think you're in any danger?"

Cattle and horses were prime property. You didn't steal another man's horse. You didn't steal another man's cattle, let alone slaughter it and leave it lying in the open to rot. In many territories, such behavior could lead to a quick hanging.

"No," he said softly, stopping by the open doorway and staring out at the children as they gathered eggs in the chicken coop. "But McGregor's got the pocket watch." He glanced over his shoulder toward her. "Unfortunately, I have no idea who's behind all of this or who tried to frame me for the cattle."

"Maybe you should go talk to the sheriff."

"I intend to." He stared out the doorway for several more moments and then turned away, leaning against the threshold. "I'll have to find a job in town as well as a place for us to stay there."

Gabrielle stared at him, wishing that she could say something that would help. "From what I've seen, Aiden, the townspeople like you. I don't think they'll believe that you did any of the things that McGregor thinks you did."

"Be that as it may, Gabrielle, we no longer have a roof over our heads." He glanced upward at the ceiling. "Nor do I presently have a job, and chances are that it's going to be difficult to get one, after these accusations against me make the rounds."

"The Lord will provide," she said quietly. Why was this happening to them now? The girls were just starting to trust her, and while she wished that things were a bit better between her and Aiden, she had seen a little bit of progress there. Household chores were still very difficult, but she was healing.

"Well, I guess I best be going. I can talk to Jake about maybe helping him around the mercantile, or maybe he knows someone who's looking for help."

Gabrielle looked up. "I can help too, Aiden." She didn't miss the doubtful glance he sent her way, focusing on her hands. "I can tutor children," she rushed on, growing more confident as she thought about it. "I was a smart student back home and I often helped the schoolteacher in her classroom, when I could get away from the bakery." Her eyes widened. "I'm an excellent baker too, and I can start making baked goods to sell."

He smiled down at her. "I appreciate your enthusiasm, Gabrielle, but we both know that even being around heat bothers your hands still."

She waved him off. "I can find a way to get around that." She looked up at him, her eyes wide and a smile on her lips. "We can do this, Aiden! We can. Maybe I can even help you save a little more so that you can buy that ranch you want."

Aiden stepped toward her and placed his hands on her shoulders, looking deep into her eyes. "You're something, you know that?"

He bent down and kissed her gently on the lips. Startled, Gabrielle only stood there, not sure what to do. His lips felt warm and soft against hers, and though the kiss only lasted a brief moment, she knew she wanted more where that came from. He gazed down at her with a slight frown wrinkling his forehead, as if he were surprised by his actions.

She smiled up at him. "Where there's a will, there's a way." To her surprise, he wrapped his arms around her again and gave her a gentle hug. She wrapped her own arms around his waist, feeling the strength of him, smelling the scent of horse and rich earth in his clothes. For the first time in a very long while, she felt safe.

Two days later, Aiden, Gabrielle, and the girls moved to an upstairs room of the mercantile. When Jake learned what had happened, he swore up one side and down the other about Mike McGregor and his foolish notions, and then immediately offered the space for the family. It was tight quarters, no doubt, but it would do temporarily.

Jake and Aiden resituated the stocks and supplies downstairs while Gabrielle and the girls did the best they could to make the cramped space a temporary home. All they could bring upstairs were their straw-filled mattresses. The bed frames were broken down and stored. The kitchen table was shoved into one corner, a rocking chair in the other, Gabrielle and Aiden's mattress in one corner, the girls sharing a mattress in the other.

It wasn't ideal, far from it. It was hot and stuffy up on the second floor, with only two small windows to offer ventilation. No doorway closed off the stairs that led up, so they would be privy to all the transactions, noise, and negotiations going on downstairs.

Gabrielle knew that Aiden didn't want to feel beholden to Jake for offering the space. He wanted to find other living arrangements as soon as possible. He was going around town at the moment, looking to hire on somewhere, not too proud to take anything that was offered. He had to put food on the table. As far as that went, he would also spread the word about Gabrielle's ability to tutor, and Gabrielle, after straightening up their new living quarters, contemplated how she could start baking.

Of course there was no stove up here, but there was a small potbellied stove downstairs in the corner of the mercantile, keeping the place warm in winter. Maybe if she worked it out right, she could prepare delicacies upstairs, then take them down and bake them, one at a time as she had to, downstairs. The girls had already offered to help.

What she really needed was a good, heavy, thick pair of oven mitts that would help protect her hands and arms from the heat of the stove, now and into the future. She had met the town's seamstress, who owned a small millinery, and queried her about the cost to fashion such an item for her. The woman had graciously offered to craft a pair for her in exchange for credit in the form of two pies, two dozen biscuits, and three loaves of bread.

Gabrielle turned to head back to the mercantile, her eyes brimming with tears of gratitude. She was growing to love the people of Maple Grove. While she had been close to many friends back home, this sense of pulling together, of camaraderie, was amazing, especially in light of the fact of what Aiden had been accused of. Of course, most didn't believe that Aiden was guilty of doing such a thing, and there was more than one person in town who said not so nice things about McGregor.

Because of the change in circumstances, Gabrielle wanted to put off seeing the new doctor in town, but Aiden insisted. He knew the pain she was in, even though she tried her best to hide it. Any minute now, he would be coming "home" to escort her to the new doctor's office, situated above the bank at the far end of town.

❧

WITHIN THE HOUR, THEY'D ENTERED THE DOCTOR'S small, cramped, yet surprisingly well-stocked office. A chair sat off to the side of the room, behind a curtain that could be pulled for privacy. One wall contained shelves of bottles and jars filled with powders, pill tablets, and liquids. A rolltop desk perched in the other, while the last portion of one wall was filled with a shelf of medical books.

Dr. Micah Harris was a handsome young man. Emphasis on young. He explained that he had recently graduated from medical school back east and had always wanted to come to California, so here he was. With Aiden standing over her, Gabrielle sat in the chair and removed her gloves. The young doctor stared at her hands a moment and then grimaced.

"Well, you've got some damage here, don't you?"

Gabrielle said nothing, but allowed the doctor to take her hands and test her joint mobility, her ability to rotate wrists and elbows. Then he palpated her forearms, sometimes squeezing gently into the meat of those damaged forearm muscles as she tried her best not to wince.

He had her try to perform basic dexterity exercises, like touching her index finger to her thumb. She grew frustrated and shook her head as she failed to complete even one of the exercises he gave her.

"Don't fret, Gabrielle—"

A small cough from Aiden prompted him to glance up. The doctor's cheeks colored. "Excuse me ... Mrs. Roberts." He glanced once more at Aiden before returning his attention to her. "I can give you some exercises to help relieve the growing stiffness. It'll take time, but if you do them two or three times a day, it can help stretch out the injured tendons and enable more mobility. If you don't do the exercises, the burn scars will eventually cause more contractions and you won't be able to move your fingers at all."

They left the office, Gabrielle having turned down tablets that might've eased the pain. She would try the exercises first. Medicine cost money. As they left, she glanced at Aiden. "What do you think?"

Aiden scowled. "You're already doing exercises. Granted the ones he gave you to do are different, but it sounds like some quackery to me. Let's see what happens."

Gabrielle frowned as she glanced up at her husband. She had seen the scowl on his face the moment they walked into the doctor's office and spied the young doctor. "We'll see," she agreed. "He may be young, but he seems very smart. Did you see all those books in there? And the fact that he graduated from a prestigious medical school back east? That's quite impressive. I'm pretty sure he knows what he's talking about."

Aiden didn't look down at her, but walked stiffly beside her, a hand cupping one elbow. Gabrielle's heart sank. Did he think the visit had been a waste of fifty cents? If he didn't believe that she could overcome her injuries, if he didn't support her in this, she didn't know what she would do. She had been so excited to see the doctor, but now a sensation of dread settled into the pit of her stomach.

CHAPTER 8

Two weeks passed, weeks during which Aiden grew increasingly frustrated and dissatisfied. Though many of the townspeople wanted to help, and though none of those he honestly spoke with believed he could be responsible for the odd things going on around Maple Grove, there just weren't that many steady jobs available in town. He helped out where he could, earning a bit of money here and there, but for the most part, it was a day-by-day situation.

Gabrielle had been a bit more fortunate in that she found some tutoring work with several of the children in town. While Maple Grove was fairly modern, it had yet to build a schoolhouse. The bit of money that Gabrielle earned combined with what Aiden earned got them by with food, but very little to offer Jake in return for using the space above his mercantile.

Aiden's pride was injured, but that wasn't his only problem. In his mind, his gradually developing relationship with Gabrielle had been threatened. By the young doctor no less. Gabrielle waxed enthusiastic about the young doctor and the exercises he had given her to do. Every evening at their small supper table, she showed Aiden what she could do after only a few days. A barely perceptible improvement in her ability to bend an index finger, in her efforts to touch a thumb to her pinky, and while Aiden tried to smile and offer encouragement, he felt a heaviness in his heart that he couldn't deny. It was the doctor who'd helped Gabrielle. Not Aiden. It was the doctor offering her hope. Not Aiden. He couldn't even give her a proper home.

It wasn't just jealousy. It was a worry that maybe he had failed to make a proper connection to Gabrielle. That her injuries and her lack of abilities had held him back from really making a great enough effort. The new doctor's attention and his praise wasn't helping any.

"I'm going to be working at the mill today, helping Jamie load grain for shipment," he said, setting his coffee mug down on the table as he watched Gabrielle gather the children's plates, littered with leftover scrambled eggs and bacon.

"That's good," she said, smiling. "I don't have any children to tutor today, so I'm going to spend extra time doing my exercises." Her eyes shone with hope. "I think they're helping, Aiden, I really think that Dr. Harris is right, that the more I do these exercises, the more I use my fingers and hands, the better I'll do!"

He loved her smile. It lit up her entire face, warming his heart. And yet Aiden frowned. It had been difficult to have any sort of conversation with Gabrielle with all of them living together without any privacy, but at this moment the children were out back behind the mercantile, playing. He heard their occasional squeals of laughter and wished he could be so happy and carefree again.

"Gabrielle, try not to get your hopes up too much," he said softly. He knew the doctor was trying to be encouraging, but he couldn't help but feel he was raising his wife's hopes to unattainable goals.

"What do you mean?"

He sighed. "Look, I just don't want you to get your hopes up too much." He glanced at her hands, her forearms hidden under the sleeves of her blouse. "You received a lot of damage and ..."

"And what?" Gabrielle asked, a frown appearing on her own brow.

"Look, I understand that the doctor's doing what he feels best to keep your spirits up, but I think you also have to be realistic too."

Gabrielle set the dishes she'd been gathering down on the table with a loud *thunk*. "What are you trying to say, Aiden?"

He was mad at the doctor, he was mad at McGregor for firing him, he was mad that he couldn't provide for his family and had to rely on other's goodwill and partly on his wife's earnings just to put food on the table. He spoke without thought. "What I'm trying to say, Gabrielle, is that you might not be able to do everything you want to do. You might not be able to accomplish as much as my Sarah did in the short time she had on earth, but you have to adapt, sooner or later."

"Are you expecting me to take the place of your first wife? Of Sarah? I would never presume to do so!" She straightened as her voice rose slightly. "I'm not Sarah, Aiden. I'm Gabrielle Dawson Roberts! I'm the woman married to you!" She lifted her scarred hands. "Despite my limitations, I'm doing the best I can to be a proper wife and stepmother to your children, and if you can't see that, well, that's your fault, not mine!"

He saw the color drain from Gabrielle's face and realized what he'd said ... *my Sarah* ... He'd hurt her deeply. He couldn't take it back. Aiden swallowed. "I'm sorry, Gabrielle, I didn't mean it that way. It didn't ... it didn't come out the way I meant it to."

She said nothing, but simply turned and walked away from him, heading down the stairs. Through the small window, he saw her striding stiffly away from the store toward the other side of town. With a sigh, Aiden rose and went downstairs himself, thinking to follow her until he saw Jake calmly rearranging one-pound bags of sugar on a counter.

"You did it this time, didn't you?" Jake grinned, an eyebrow lifted.

Aiden scowled. "What do you mean? Did you hear us talking up there?"

Jake shook his head. "No, but I saw the look on her face as she stomped downstairs." He gestured with his thumb over shoulder. "I think she's headed over to the livery stable."

Aiden moved past him toward the rear door but Jake clasped his arm and shook his head. "You better give her some space before you try to talk to her."

Aiden looked at his friend. "Being a lifelong bachelor, who suddenly made you such an expert on wives and marriage?"

Jake chuckled. "Thankfully, I'm not, so it's easy to dispense advice. But I know angry when I see it." He glanced around the store. "I'm not going to open for another hour, but I've got an errand to run so I'll be away for a while ..." he grinned again. "If you want to talk and make up."

Aiden shook his head with impatience. "I've got to get over to the mill to help Jamie."

With that, they parted ways, and Aiden headed to the mill, frustrated by his present circumstances. He wanted to go after Gabrielle, to apologize for what he'd said, but he had to get to work, such as it was.

Of course he regretted what he had said. He had to stop comparing Gabrielle with Sarah. He couldn't replace Sarah, and he didn't intend to. He wasn't sure what disturbed him to such degree. He had simply spoken the truth about Gabrielle's hopes with her hands. He'd not meant to hurt her. He felt he'd grown closer to Gabrielle over the past weeks, hoping and praying that she'd warm up to him. If they could just get past a few challenges, he felt certain that they would get along just fine.

They had both been dealt tragedies, and while Aiden always accepted God's blessings for what he had, he also had to learn to accept when things didn't go just right. He had to trust in the Lord. "Uphold my steps in your paths, that my footsteps not slip," he murmured. He tried to live a godly life. He tried to be a good man. So if the Lord felt he needed to work harder at it, he would.

Bad things happened. It was how people dealt with those tragedies, how Gabrielle dealt with those tragedies, how Aiden responded to them, that mattered. Her faith was strong. He had to be as strong in faith as well. While his feelings for Gabrielle had slowly developed and he respected her immensely for her determination to get past not only her grief, but her physical limitations, he was the one focusing on them. Aiden was the one focused on the "what ifs." What if she couldn't use her hands to their fullest capabilities? What if she continued to struggle with the simplest of chores? Things like laundry, cooking for the children, and sewing?

He realized where his thoughts strayed and barely bit back a curse. He should be ashamed. Gabrielle was more than a maid. If she couldn't manage sewing, they could hire someone to do sewing for them. He could help more with the laundry and the cooking. He had been doing that since Sarah died anyway, hadn't he?

"You're a fool." Shame filled him. Gabrielle was a beautiful, kindhearted woman who had accepted his children without reservations. So why hadn't he given her the same considerations? His children had warmed up to Gabrielle, and after their initial fear over her scars, were now open and willing to help her in any way they could. Why hadn't he shown her the same courtesy?

Aiden resolved to make it up to her tonight. She was trying to move on from her own tragedy. She, like him, had faced loss and still grieved. Instead of criticizing her efforts to improve her physical capabilities, he should've been more enthusiastic. He vowed to make it right. Somehow.

CHAPTER 9

Gabrielle headed for the far side of town, toward the livery stables, not sure why. Her anger had burgeoned over Aiden's words, then morphed into sadness and dismay. She needed to get away from him, away from the mercantile and its cramped quarters to gather her thoughts. She sensed Aiden pulling away from her and believed that maybe he didn't want to be married to her anymore. Lately, he'd been short-tempered and seemingly unhappy with his life.

He never said it, but she wondered if he in some way blamed her for the pressures on him now. No, that couldn't be it. She was just one more mouth to feed. He would've had to make the same decision about moving into town whether she was here or not. He had to provide shelter, food, and clothing for the children.

Her heart breaking, Gabrielle wondered if she should just leave and go back home, where people honestly loved her. The marriage hadn't been consummated, so an annulment shouldn't be a huge difficulty. The problem was getting back home. She had no money for that and neither did Aiden. He was saving for property of his own, but she would never ask him to use that for any other purpose.

She shook her head, wandering around the livery toward the corral outside where a half-dozen horses stood lazily in the midmorning sunshine, their tails swishing at flies. One moved over to the fence and Gabrielle stroked its muzzle, threading her fingers through its mane.

What to do? She was very hurt by Aiden's words, and though she didn't believe that he had meant the words to come out the way they had, she had to make him look at her as Gabrielle. Not Sarah. She was his wife now. She would be a mother to his children as best she could.

She would—

A hint of smoke wafted toward her and she froze, a chill racing down her spine. The mere hint of it instilled a sense of panic inside her, bringing with it the memories of that horrible night. Not a cooking fire, not the scent of wood burning in a stove. It carried a sharp aroma with it, like kerosene, but ...

Suddenly, a flame burst through the rear window of the livery, a rising black tendril of smoke behind it, hovering over the structure. The horses began to mill about, alarmed and snorting, their hooves prancing as they circled.

"Fire!" Gabrielle cried, her voice barely carrying beyond the corral.

Nothing happen. Where was the livery owner? She glanced around, saw no one, and stared in horror as the flames grew larger, taller, and hungrier. A breeze picked up embers and carried it toward another structure about twenty feet away. The barbershop. In seconds, flames appeared there too, along the ridge of the shop. As if attracted by something pulling them in that direction, devouring dry shingling, then moving down, hungry for wood or anything to propel the flames.

Gabrielle screamed for help once more and then quickly turned toward the corral, looking for the gate. Not caring whether the owner got upset, she opened the gate and let the horses loose. They ran toward a nearby meadow, ears flicking, nostrils flaring, eyes wide with fear at the flames now consuming half the stable and the hay stored inside.

"Fire!" Gabrielle screamed, turning to find that the flames now raced along the rooflines of several other structures, threatening to engulf the entire town. But why? How? The breeze wasn't *that* strong ...

Her screams finally alerted several inhabitants of town and storekeepers and business owners rushed out their doors, looking around wildly. In moments, a bucket brigade started to form on the eastern edge of town.

Gabrielle looked toward the western side of town, down along Main Street, and saw with alarm and a shiver of dread how quickly the flames were moving. It was as if someone had doused every structure with kerosene—

Oh no ... was that how the fire started? Why it was moving so quickly? But who would do—

She froze, eyes wide with alarm, heart pounding. The mercantile! The mercantile was on fire! The children were no longer playing behind it. Had they gone back upstairs? She heard several small pops. Seconds later, glass flew from several windows of nearby structures, burst out by the heat of flames inside. Gabrielle turned away from them and hurried toward the mercantile. Gray smoke already oozed from between the boards on the lower floor.

No!

She picked up her skirts and ran, heart racing, her blood chilled despite the warmth of the morning. No, this couldn't be happening again! She watched, confused as townspeople rushed past her in the opposite direction, hurrying to form a fire brigade to deal with the fires closer to the livery. Men shouted orders and women joined the throng of townspeople racing to save the structures from burning completely to the ground. Men with buckets raced toward water troughs, while women ran toward the small stream and pond behind the structures, lugging back filled buckets, water sloshing over their rims, eyes wide with fear and determination.

Gabrielle raced toward the mercantile, calling the children's names. "Rebecca! Mary!" She paused maybe twenty feet from the structure to look up at the small window of their quarters. With horror, she spied Rebecca, screaming and pounding at the glass.

"O Lord, please, don't them die. Help me save them!"

Despite her terror, Gabrielle raced into the mercantile, almost immediately driven back by flames and heat and smoke. It crackled, seemingly laughing at her efforts. She nearly doubled over as she took in a lungful of smoke, but refused to give up. She had to get to the children! She made her way through small areas of flame inside the store, consuming Jake's products, aiming for the stairs. She must save the children, regardless of any danger to herself. She couldn't fail like she had failed to save her parents.

With one arm braced in front of her, the heat already causing her forearms and hands to tingle with pain, Gabrielle tried to cover her mouth and nose, moving ever closer to the stairs.

"Gabrielle!"

She heard the scream from above and looked up at the doorway to find Rebecca standing at the top, holding Mary close to her, both of them terrified, Mary's face streaked with tears.

"I'm coming!" she managed to cry. "I'm coming!"

The fire moved incredibly quickly, the dry tinder of the siding smoking one moment and erupting with flames the next. The heat nearly unbearable, Gabrielle took the steps upward, avoiding the banister, already smoking. Flames licked up the far wall of the store. If that wall collapsed, the entire structure would fall upon them. She stumbled and went down on her knees, crying out at the sharp pain as her knee collided with a step riser. The steps themselves grew hot.

How could the fire move so quickly? How had a mere breeze sent a fire through town so quickly? Over the increasing roar of angry flames, the crackling and the popping, the hiss of smoke as it *whooshed* through openings fed by air, Gabrielle glanced quickly around, her attention momentarily captured by blue flames erupting from the packages of sugar Jake had been stacking carefully on the counter as she had left in a huff just a short while earlier.

"Gabrielle!"

She looked up and saw Mary sagging slowly downward in Rebecca's grasp, Rebecca herself coughing and gasping for air. "I'm coming!" she tried to tell the girls, but her voice was a hoarse croak.

Her ears rang as she sought fresh air where none was to be found. Outside, shouts of alarm grew fainter. The sound of the flames grew louder. Those flames were alive, waiting to consume her, as they probably should have back home in the bakery in Missouri. She stumbled once more, her feet catching in the bottom of her skirt. *No! Keep going. You have to reach the children ...*

She finally reached the top of the stairs and grabbed Mary with her left arm, ignoring the pain that caused her head to spin as she clutched the child close to her. She grabbed Rebecca's hand and quickly urged them down the stairs. Rebecca pulled back.

"No, Gabrielle! I'm scared!"

With a strength born of fear, she urged Rebecca down the stairs with her, Mary's weight pulling against her injured arm, prompting her shoulder to burn, not with fire, but with exertion. The child was limp and she could only pray that she was still alive.

"Come!" Gabrielle managed, glancing at Rebecca, tightly clasping her free hand, so very tightly she thought she couldn't stand the pain for one more second. But she hung on. She grasped the precious children closer to her, refusing to let the flames have them.

Not this time.

CHAPTER 10

Aiden worked behind the mill, between the rear of the stone structure and a stream that ran along the back end of town before curling out into the valley. He paused with a frown when he caught a hint of smoke in the air. He glanced up but didn't see anything. He finished tying off the heavy burlap sack now filled with grain and heaved it onto his shoulders to carry inside, to add it to the pile that would soon be loaded into a wagon for delivery at a nearby ranch.

He'd barely placed the sack on the floor with a quiet thud when Jamie approached. "Jamie, do you smell that?"

Jamie lifted his nose into the air once more and sniffed, then cast Aiden a frown, eyes narrowed. "Smells like fire."

Aiden paused, smelled the air as well, and agreed. His heart skipped a beat and he moved outside to the front of the grain mill and froze. At the opposite end of town he saw a curl of smoke rising. "Jamie, look!"

The two of them stared a moment, stunned as grayish white smoke fire rose into the air. Aiden blinked as the first flames shot up into the sky.

"Something is on fire!" Jamie shouted, running out the mill and down the street.

Aiden followed, heart racing, fear tingling down his spine at the thought of one of the town structures on fire. In this dry weather, the wood structures were vulnerable, and it would only take—

Jamie ran ahead of him, shouting to the townspeople, although from the amount of people running out into the street, most were clearly already aware of the danger. Aiden ran past the boarding house when he heard a shout. He skidded to a stop and turned to find old man Vickers waving desperately.

"Aiden! Aiden, come help me with Mabel!"

Though Aiden desperately wanted to follow Jamie, to help put out the fire and to check on Gabrielle and the children, he hurried toward the old man. Jeremy Vickers was in his early eighties, and his wife, seventy-eight-year-old Mabel, was confined to a wheelchair from some kind of wasting disease. Vickers struggled to push the wooden wheelchair with the wicker backing out the door but one of the wheels kept getting stuck on the threshold. Poor Mabel sat there, wide-eyed with fright, clinging to the arms of the wheelchair, leaning forward as if trying to help her husband.

"Wait, Jeremy, wait." Aiden raced to the door. "You're not going to make it that way." He glanced down at Mabel and then back at Jeremy. "You mind?"

"Not at all, son," Jeremy said.

Aiden turned to Mabel. "Missus Vickers, I'm going to lift you out of the chair and carry you to the edge of the yard so Jeremy can get the wheelchair out the door. Okay?"

She didn't say a word, but reached her hands toward Aiden. He bent and easily lifted the old woman into his arms. She was little more than skin and bones and he quickly hurried to the edge of the yard with her, cradling her in his arms as he looked to the east end of town.

"Hurry, Jeremy!" he shouted. "Buildings are on fire and it's spreading fast!"

His heart pounding with terror, Aiden wanted desperately to get Mabel taken care of so that he could check on Gabrielle and his children at the mercantile. As fast as the fire was spreading, the whole town could go up in no time. "Hurry, Jeremy!"

In moments, Jeremy had managed to wrestle the wheelchair out the door and quickly push it toward Aiden. He gently set Mabel in the chair and then looked back up at Jeremy, pointing toward the edge of town. "Take shelter over there," he said.

He didn't wait for Jeremy's reply before he was off and running down Main Street. He heard the flames now, cracking and popping, the sound of glass breaking, the *whoosh* of fire as the flames found fuel. Eyes wide as he ran, his gaze sweeping the street, seeking signs of Gabrielle and the children, Aiden realized that the livery at the far edge of town was completely engulfed. The barbershop, the seamstress store, and several other structures were smoking and burning.

He heard a shout. "The gunsmith shop! Stay away! Everybody *stay away*!"

Suddenly, the ground shook once as the gunsmith shop exploded, sending a ball of roiling fire into the air. A black ball of smoke rose upward as the gunpowder stored in barrels exploded once more. Bullets popped as townspeople scattered, racing away from the structure, one man crying out as he was hit by a flying piece of shrapnel or maybe a bullet. He fell, grabbing his shoulder. Two men raced to his aid, dragging him with them as they ran to a safer distance.

Shouts, screams, warnings all blended together, coupled with the sound of orders shouted by the sheriff and others who had started the bucket brigade.

"Aiden! Over here!"

He gazed frantically around and realize that it was Jamie calling to him, thrusting a bucket toward him. "Come on! We can stop it from spreading if we—"

A scream interrupted, and Aiden froze, searching the street once more. He gaze landed on the mercantile. Smoke curled from the roof and threaded its grayish-black fingers through some of the seams of the structure. The children! A groan erupted from his throat as he headed for the store. He couldn't see the children, couldn't find

Gabrielle. Had the children gone back inside or were they safe and sound? He had to—

He nearly stumbled to a halt when he saw Gabrielle rushing toward the mercantile, her skirts held high, hair disheveled.

"Gabrielle!" Aiden shouted, his voice tinged with panic and fear. *No!* Too late, he watched her disappear through the rear door into the structure just as flames emerged from the front. "Gabrielle, stop!" he shouted to no avail.

He raced forward, eyes focused on the now burning structure, trying to anticipate his moves once he reached it. He had to save Gabrielle and the children. Aiden was across the street from the structure when a hand grabbed his arm and held him back, so forcefully he nearly lost his footing. He glanced frantically over his shoulder, trying to push away whoever was holding him.

"Aiden!"

"Jake!" Aiden shouted, his voice cracking with panic as he pointed. "Gabrielle's in there. The children!"

Jake stared at the burning structure. "I'll get some men over here with water—"

"No time! She's in there, she's—"

A child's scream pierced the air. Aiden's heart froze with a terror such as he'd never felt before, consuming him much like the flames consuming the structure. *O Lord, no, please...*

"Becca!" he cried, fighting back his fear, a fear that nearly buckled his knees. He turned to Jake, his eyes stinging with smoke. He struggled against Jake's grasp. "Let me go, Jake!"

Jake did, turning quickly to shout for help while Aiden approached the mercantile, the smoke acrid, stinging and scorching his nostrils and his lungs. He reached the open threshold, where the heat emanating from the structure battered him. He stepped inside, one hand lifted in front of his face, as if that would ward off the flames. Aiden heard crying from up the stairs and looked up to find Gabrielle at the top, reaching for the children.

She lifted Mary into her arms, clasping her to her side with one arm, grasping Rebecca's hand with the other and starting down the stairs.

"Papa!" Rebecca screamed.

He heard no sound from Mary or Gabrielle. He had to get to them! Aiden moved toward the stairs just as part of the ceiling at the front of the store collapsed, sending embers everywhere. He felt their stinging pain as they ate through his shirt, singed his hair, and landed on his skin.

"Hurry!" he shouted, pushing through the smoke, his squinted eyes narrowed against the sting, watering almost to the point he couldn't see. The heat surrounding him was hot and greedy, flames shooting up from the floor now, reaching for him. Aiden was only ten feet away from the base of the stairs when another rumbling crash shook the building. Shelves collapsed. Upstairs, he heard a groan, timbers strained to their limit, weakened by the heat.

He heard a cry. "... her!"

"Gabrielle!"

"Take her," he heard. A second later, an unconscious Mary was thrust into his arms. Aiden took her and tried to reach for Gabrielle or Rebecca, shouting their names over the sound of the flames.

He heard Rebecca scream, followed by a thudding sound. "Rebecca!"

Coughing, gagging on acrid smoke, he felt a small hand grasp the waistband of his pants.

"Papa!"

"Gabrielle!" he shouted. Just then, there was another crash, followed by the collapse of the stairs. He heard a scream, abruptly cut off. Rebecca tugged on his arm. Mary still limp in the other, he felt another hand on his back.

"Aiden, give the children to me!"

Jake. Aiden quickly thrust Mary into his arms, took Rebecca's hand, and despite her best efforts to resist, peeled her fingers off his wrist. "Go with Jake!" he shouted, barely managing that without breaking down into a fit of coughs. He could hardly breathe, the air filled with soot and smoke. His lungs burned. "Go!"

Aiden counted on Jake to get the children out while he moved forward, arms outstretched, seeking Gabrielle. No, he couldn't lose her, not now, and not like this. She'd risked her life to save his children and he wouldn't let her die in here.

"Gabrielle!" he shouted one more time, then nearly tripped over something on the floor. He stumbled and fell to his knees, thrusting out a hand to stop his forward momentum. He hissed in pain as his hand came into contact with a glowing timber. With his left hand, he braced himself on the floor as he struggled to rise.

His heart pounding so hard it was a wonder it didn't burst, he retreated to his hands and knees and quickly crawled along the floor, following the fabric until he realized that it was Gabrielle's skirt. She lay prone on the floor. A smoldering beam lay on top of her. His heart sank.

"Gabrielle!" he shouted once more, grasping the wooden beam, and struggling to his feet, strained to lift the beam off of her.

"Go, Aiden," she cried. "Save the children!" She broke down into a fit of coughing.

"They're safe," he told her, fighting the smoke, trying to ignore the heat of the flames surrounding them. "They're going to be all right. Hold on, I'll get you out of here!"

"Go, Aiden!" she cried. "The children need you!"

He strained to lift the beam, his muscles bulging, his hands singed, pain shooting up his arms. "The children need *us*!" With every ounce of strength he had, he managed to move the beam off her just as another crash came from upstairs. Without hesitation, he grabbed Gabrielle by the arms, dragging her toward the rear threshold of the mercantile just as a chunk of the ceiling crashed down where she had lain only seconds before.

Panting for breath, his vision fading, his legs wobbled precariously. It took everything Aiden had to lift Gabrielle into his arms. He straightened, orienting himself. He could only pray that he was heading in the right direction, flames surrounding him as he struggled to carry Gabrielle through the mercantile, over glowing timbers, flames licking up the sides of the structure, sending embers and clouds of billowing smoke around him.

He stumbled once, nearly dropping Gabrielle, but he forged on. It seemed like forever and he began to lose hope that he would save either himself or Gabrielle. Just then, hands reached for him. Despite his protests, they pulled Gabrielle out of his arms while others grabbed his. Finally, he emerged from the structure, coughing and exhausted.

The townspeople raced about, struggling to save what structures they could, leaving those that were too badly damaged to save to burn as they focused on saving the others. Aiden saw Gabrielle lying in the middle of the street, surrounded by several others, his girls huddled close by, tears streaking their cheeks as the town's seamstress tried to comfort them. Relief flitted through Aiden when he saw that his children were all right. He turned to Gabrielle, his heart skipping a beat when he saw her lying unmoving. Doc Harris leaned over her, holding her limp wrist in his hand, checking for a pulse.

Nearly doubled over, his hands burning, his lungs gasping for air, Aiden sank down beside his children and pulled them into his arms, his eyes never leaving Gabrielle's. He stared at her, willing her to live, stunned by her bravery and her act of selflessness. She had risked her life to save his children. Their children. An overwhelming surge of emotion filled his heart, bringing more tears to his eyes. He had fallen in love with her. Without even realizing it, he had fallen in love with this determined woman who refused to be broken by the tragedies she had endured.

He reached for her hand, her scarred, wonderful hand, and lifted it to his lips. "I love you, Gabrielle," he said. "I love you."

Doc Harris looked up at him, then offered a nod. "I'm taking her to my office. She breathed in a lot of smoke and has a couple of broken ribs, but she's breathing, her pulse is strong, and I'm confident that she'll recover."

Aiden pulled his weeping children to him, holding them close, all of them smelling of smoke, a strong surge of relief rushing through him as he looked down at his girls. "She's going to be all right, girls. She's going to be all right."

Jake helped him to his feet and steadied him when his knees threatened to collapse beneath him. The girls desperately clung to Aiden's hands as Cody and Jamie carried Gabrielle toward the doctor's office. Murmurs of support followed Aiden and the girls as they followed, and tears of gratitude filled his eyes. A fire might have destroyed half of Maple Grove, but it hadn't destroyed the spirits of the people who lived here. Their generosity, gratitude, and friendship could never be destroyed.

"Come on, girls. Doc will take care of Gabrielle and then make sure that you're both all right too."

Mary looked up at him. "You told Gabby that you loved her."

Gabby. Aiden's child looked up at him with a soot-smudged face. "That I did, honey, that I did."

Mary scrunched up her face. "Do you think she knows that we love her too?"

Aiden fought back a lump in his throat as he smiled down at his daughter and nodded. "I'm sure she does, Mary."

EPILOGUE

AIDEN WATCHED WITH A SMILE AS REBECCA AND MARY playing with a gaggle of other children cavorting beneath the shade of two young maple trees in their yard. Nearly a month had passed since the fire had nearly destroyed Maple Grove. Through sheer determination, the towns-people had managed to save about half of it.

The sheriff said the fire was deliberate. He had found kerosene jugs scattered behind the structures that had burned, more behind those that didn't. The discovery was sobering to everyone. Who would set the town on fire? And why?

After the fire was put out, the remains of several structure still smoldering, the scent of smoke and destruction heavy in the air, Aiden sat in a chair in front of the doctor's office, staring down at his bandaged hands. They'd been mildly burned, not nearly as badly as Gabrielle's had been in the fire that had taken her parents' lives. It was only then, staring down at his own aching hands that Aiden realized what Gabrielle had gone through, how hard she had tried to recover after her devastating injuries.

He hadn't understood her pain, her frustration, until he himself had gotten his hands singed pulling her from beneath that beam. And yet, his injuries weren't even close to hers. The thought brought a lump of emotion to his throat.

Doc Harris had assured Aiden that Gabrielle would recover, and she had. While the fire was a devastating event, it had also resulted in some joy. For one, Aiden and Gabrielle resolved to never withhold their feelings from one another. While Gabrielle healed, staying at Doc Harris's makeshift hospital where he cared for her and others injured in the fire, Aiden and the children stayed in the old, original soddy on Cody Maxwell's farm, though that ended up only being a temporary arrangement.

The day after the fire, his former boss, rancher Mike McGregor, approached him, hat in hand, mumbling his apologies for accusing Aiden of perpetrating thievery and killing his cattle. Everyone knew that it would've been impossible for Aiden to start the fire in the livery stable at one end of town when he was filling grain sacks at the other, so his name was officially cleared—not that anyone really believed that he had been responsible for any of the odd incidents that had been occurring in the area for the past several months.

McGregor felt so bad about his accusations against Aiden that he paid him a bonus and told him if he'd accept it, he'd pay off half of Aiden's balance for the purchase of the property he'd had his heart set on for so long. Aiden gratefully accepted, and only a day later, a dozen men from town showed up in their wagons, loaded with tools, lumber, and grins. Women brought baskets of food. Within a day, the frame of his house was constructed, along with half a barn. In less than a week, the house and barn were ready to move in.

On move-in day, McGregor gifted him with half dozen cattle, while Cody Maxwell gave Aiden and Gabrielle a milk cow, and yet another nearby rancher gave the couple three horses; a stallion, a gelding, and a pregnant mare. Other items including furniture, curtains, and dishware were given as belated wedding presents to the couple.

Now, a couple of weeks later, still settling into their new home, Gabrielle rushed about, preparing for the picnic she had arranged to show her gratitude to the townspeople. In town, things were bustling, the sawmill running nearly nonstop from dawn to dusk, the sound of hammers and saws and laughter ringing out as the townspeople rebuilt. Everyone shared what they had with others.

Of course they still wondered who had set the fire. What was going on in Maple Grove? Who wanted to destroy the town and its people? Still, they moved on. They rebuilt. The sheriff investigated, but today ... today was about community. It was about support and caring. While Aiden heard snatches of conversation about the fire, he heard more about how the town would grow bigger and stronger after what happened. The townspeople had pulled together like never before.

"This is nice."

Aiden turned to find Jake moving to stand beside him, staring at the people from Maple Grove, celebrating life. "That it is," Aiden nodded.

"I actually meant that everything that you've got, Aiden. A new and loving wife, your kids, your ranch ... your dreams came true, didn't they?"

Aiden nodded. "Yes, they did," he said, turning to his friend. "Thank you for supporting me."

"Soon it will be your turn to support me," Jake grinned.

Aiden looked at him with a lifted eyebrow. "What did you do?"

Jake chuckled, his hands stuffed into his pockets. "I placed an ad in the *Sacramento Bee* for a mail order bride. Yesterday."

Aiden laughed as Jake moved off without waiting for a comment. He smiled and watched half a dozen women from town bustle about, carrying things from the house to the picnic tables that had been set outside. Aiden watched, shaking his head in wonder at the organized chaos, smiling as Gabrielle appeared in the doorway. She didn't wear her gloves any longer, not afraid to show her scars in public. She kept working on her exercises, with the encouragement of Aiden and Doc Harris. The doctor had told her that if she kept up the good work, she could possibly regain nearly full recovery of her hand functions within a year.

Aiden stood underneath the shade of the maple tree, smiling at the sight of Gabrielle in the doorway, a slight breeze tugging at her hair as she gazed around at the activity. Her eyes found Aiden and she walked toward him, her smile broadening. He extended his arms and she sank into them, his arms enveloping her, holding her close. He had almost lost her and his children. Every day he thanked God for saving them.

Gabrielle lifted herself on her toes and kissed him, right in front of everybody. Aiden lifted an eyebrow and smiled down at her. "Your eyes are twinkling. I didn't know that eyes could twinkle like that."

"They can when you're happy."

His smile deepened. "Are my own eyes twinkling?"

"They will when I tell you the good news."

He chuckled. "More good news?" He gestured to the house, the barn, and the activity going on around them. "What more can a man ask for?" He meant it. "I've been blessed."

"And you're to be blessed once more," she said softly.

He gazed down at her. "I am?"

"You are," Gabrielle said, reaching for his hand and placing it on her belly. "We're going to have a child, Aiden," she murmured, looking up at him.

He stared at her for several moments, stunned with the news, and then he laughed with joy.

"See, I told you so," she replied impishly. "Your eyes are twinkling."

To **continue enjoying** Dreaming Brides of California Romance. Please check below

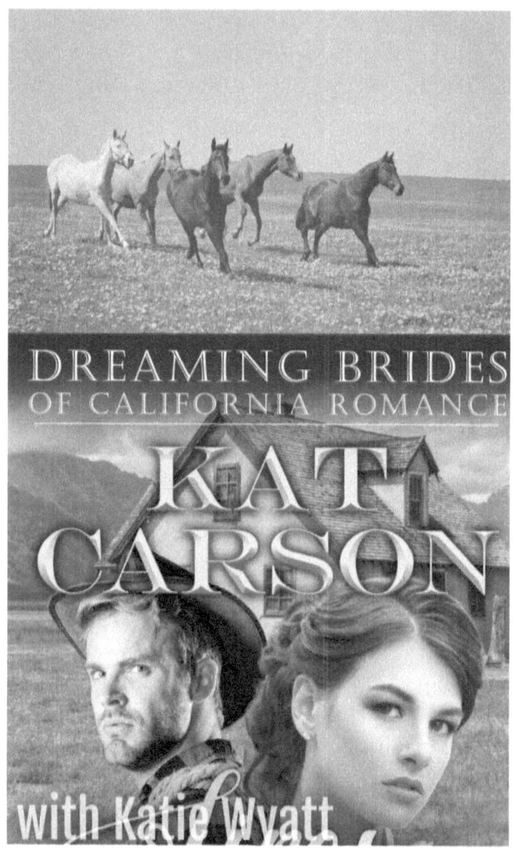

Kat Carson Dreaming Brides of California Romance

Royce Cardiff Publishing House presents other wonderful clean, wholesome and inspiring romance short stories titles for your entertainment. Many are value boxset and as always FREE to Kindle Unlimited readers.

COMPLETE SERIES
Sweet Western Romance

KATIE WYATT, BRENDA CLEMMONS AND ELLEN ANDERSON

Katie Wyatt box set complete series

Katie Wyatt Mega Box Set Series

Thank you so much for reading our book. We sincerely hope you enjoyed every bit reading it. We had fun creating it and will surely create more.

Your positive reviews are very helpful to other reader, it only takes a few moments. They can be left at Amazon.

https://www.amazon.com/Kat-Carson/e/B01G333YP0

WANT FREE BOOKS EVERY WEEK? WHO DOESN'T!

Become a preferred reader and we'll not only send you free reads, but you'll also receive updates about new releases.

So you'll be among the first to dive into our latest new books, full of adventure, heartwarming romances, and characters so real they jump off the page.

It's absolutely free and you don't need to do anything at all to qualify except go to.

PREFERRED READ FREE READS

http:/katieWyattBooks.com/readersgroup

Kat Carson lives in New Mexico with her two dogs, a horse, and 20 chickens. She started writing when she was a teenager and has never stopped. She loves the rich culture of the old West.

Some of her stories are inspired by tales from the local storytellers in New Mexico and what her grandparents used to tell her. Others are when she travels around in her RV camping, fishing, hiking, climbing and engaging with other interesting people along the way.

She writes stories derived from actual historical facts and events and sometimes individuals with interesting characters in nature that will captivate you and leave you in awe with the twists and turns of every story.

Packed with action, humor, challenge, and adventure her short stories will stretch the limits of your imagination, allowing you to marvel at the fascinating time in US history.

I recommend them for anybody who enjoys an excellent feel good clean and wholesome romance story.

KATIE WYATT IS 25% AMERICAN SIOUX INDIAN. BORN and raised in Arizona, she has traveled and camped extensively through California, Arizona, Nevada, Mexico, and New Mexico. Looking at the incredible night sky and the giant Saguaro cacti, she has dreamed of what it would be like to live in the early pioneer times.

Spending time with a relative of the great Wyatt Earp, also named Wyatt Earp, Katie was mesmerized and inspired by the stories he told of bygone times. This historical interest in the old West became the inspiration for her Western romance novels.

Her books are a mixture of actual historical facts and events mixed with action and humor, challenges and adventures. The characters in Katie's clean romance novels draw from her own experiences and are so real that they almost jump off the pages.

You feel like you're walking beside them through all the ups and downs of their lives. As the stories unfold, you'll find yourself both laughing and crying. The endings will never fail to leave you feeling warm inside.